# CHARTREUX SHOCK

# CHARTREUX SHOCK

## MARJORIE'S COZY KITTEN CAFE BOOK TWO

### KATHERINE HAYTON

Large Print Edition
ISBN: 978-1-70921-248-2

# CHAPTER ONE

Cecelia's eyes narrowed and her nostrils pinched together as she entered the café. Marjorie Hardaway—the Cozy Kitten Café owner—pulled a carrot cake muffin piled high with cream cheese icing from the display case and prepared for the same battle she'd fought with the woman once already this week.

"Can't I have my regular seat?" Cecelia asked, nodding as Marjorie checked she wanted the usual. "I love the view all the way down into the valley."

"Not when there's a customer already

sitting there." Fletcher Byrne glanced up and gave an eyeroll, forcing her to bite back a grin. "But the table by the other window is lovely, too."

"If you enjoy staring at trees," Cecelia grumbled, taking her order and flicking a dirty look in Fletcher's direction. "It would be great if we could reserve tables."

"First come, first served," Marjorie said in a light voice. "And with the work they're about to do next door, pretty soon every seat will have a clear view down the hill to the Hanmer Springs township."

The woman sniffed and took a spray bottle of hand sanitiser out of her purse. "I suppose as soon as they've cut down the trees and bushes, they'll start on building out the view altogether."

"It'll take a while before they get going," Marjorie said, déjà vu sweeping over her in a cloud. Hadn't she had the same conversation with this woman on Monday? What did Cecelia think would have changed? "At this rate, we're edging towards the foundations being poured closer to Christmas."

Monkey Business—Marjorie's Persian cat— wandered downstairs, stretching out his hind legs on every second step. His rich chocolate hairs were so fluffy, he looked enormous. Once her hands stroked the fur down, the kitten was actually on the skinnier side.

He performed an elaborate double-take while passing by Cecelia's chair, then circled around to rub himself against the table leg. She reached out a cautious finger, giving him a single stroke before returning to her coffee and cake.

A second spray with hand sanitiser sent a tingle of sadness through Marjorie's body. The poor woman couldn't last more than a few minutes before starting another cleaning ritual. It was lucky the café existed as she couldn't imagine Cecelia dealing with a full-time pet at home.

"Can I grab a refill?" Fletcher called out with an impish grin. The student had been a regular at the café for just over a month and had quickly settled into a routine. All-day, every day.

Setting the coffee machine onto his favourite latte treat, Marjorie opened the cupboard where she kept a small supply of chocolate buttons and marshmallows to adorn the saucers. A furry bundle leapt out, causing her to scream and clutch her chest.

Upon deciding it wasn't a heart attack, she scolded the small grey kitten. "Honestly, Houdini. My nerves can only take so much in one day."

The Chartreux cat shook his head and trotted over to join his friends in the play area. In the few weeks since he'd joined the kitten café, Houdini had shown a penchant for hiding in places that shouldn't be accessible or escaping from places that should have kept him contained.

"If you can't find someone to adopt him," Fletcher said, taking the latte piled high with foam out of her hands, "then you should take him on the road. Interest in human escape acts and displays of derring-do might've slowed over the years, but a kitten? Who could resist?"

He clicked his tongue at Houdini, who wandered over with a squeaky mouse from the toy pile. As he dropped it at Fletcher's feet, Marjorie thought the person most likely to adopt the rambunctious kitten was the man seated right in front of her.

"You should slow down, young man," she said, heading back to the counter. "At this rate, you'll hit your fifteen-dollar limit by lunchtime and have nothing left for the afternoon."

Claiming he missed the company of regular university life, Fletcher had set up in the café. He liked to have human, and feline, interaction while completing projects via distance learning. But, like most students, his income was fixed and non-negotiable.

Marjorie had promised to do her part to keep his tab on track with reminders, though she wouldn't go as far as turning down his custom if he broke his budget. Five years after setting up her own business, she still had trouble managing her own income.

The squeaky toy went flying across the room and Houdini gave chase, turning into a grey streak as he lunged for the mouse. Of all the kittens she'd looked after, he seemed the most dedicated hunter.

Chaplin—a creamy rag doll with an unfortunate dot of black under his pink nose —might keep watch on the birds outside from the windowsill but that was as far as he went. Bounding across the room to launch himself at the glass had been a trick it only took a few head-first smashes to cure.

"Do you have another of these carrot cake muffins?" Cecelia asked, having polished off the extravagant treat while Marjorie wasn't looking. "I might take one with me for afternoon tea."

"Sure, thing." Knowing her customer's habits, she already had one set aside in a little cardboard box. "Do you want me to ring it up now or are you staying a little longer?"

Cecelia headed for the counter. "I'd only

stay if I had a better view," she said, cueing another eyeroll from Fletcher.

Marjorie finished the transaction, then threw a paper napkin at the young man. "One of these days, you'll make me laugh and then I'll be in trouble."

"Just blame it on a kitten," Fletcher said with good-natured ease. "They're always doing something worthy of a smile."

Esme Todd burst through the double doors, her partner Jerry Menalow trailing along behind at a more languid pace. "Here're the keys," she said with a giggle. "Don't get up to anything I wouldn't do."

"Considering you pour oil on naked strangers then rub them all over, I won't get up to what you *would* do, let alone what you wouldn't." Marjorie hung the set on a hook beneath the counter, a temporary location. Only a metre off the ground made them a temptation for the kittens, like anything else in the café. "Now, give me a hug."

"We'll only be gone for a couple of weeks," Esme said with a laugh, the embrace carrying on for longer than normal. "And we're only down the road if you need us."

"I won't interrupt your first holiday in donkey's years," Marjorie protested, giving her friend a last squeeze before turning to Jerry. "And when I get around to doing the same—"

"Yeah, right." Esme gave her a light slap on the shoulder. "As if you'd ever leave this lot alone for more than a few hours at a time."

'This lot' stared at the couple with interest for a moment, before returning to their games and dozing.

"And never you mind about interrupting us." Esme slung her arm around Jerry's waist, pulling him close. "I'm sure after a few days of doing nothing, we'll both be desperate for something to fill in the time."

From the looks of them, Marjorie surmised the two of them had a perfectly good idea of how to fill it. "Now, off you get," she said, shooing them out the door. "Fletcher, can you watch the shop for a minute?"

"Sure thing."

"I hope that wasn't an open invitation for him to help himself to coffee," Esme said with another giggle. "At least if I leave someone alone in my place for a few minutes, the worst they can do is slide off the massage table onto the floor."

"Sounds like a health and safety violation waiting to happen." Marjorie pulled a cardboard box out of her apron pocket and handed it across. "I made something to keep you going on your long journey."

"I told you, it's just up the road," Jerry protested, though he took the gift of chocolate-chip biscuits willingly enough.

"Perhaps she remembers stories of your inability to ask for directions," Esme teased, her cheeks flushed with merriment. "I distinctly recall a certain someone who took four hours to get to Christchurch, even though it's a straight road from here to there."

As the two bickered, Marjorie felt a pang of regret she wasn't heading away somewhere herself. Esme was right. She wouldn't feel good leaving the kittens in anyone else's care

—no matter how capable—but her heart twisted as she remembered the beautiful scenery on the drive farther south.

The large rolling mountains would be topped with green or yellow-brown grass, depending on the season. Passing motorists would get baaed at by fat lambs growing out of their spring coats to don the thicker garb of winter. Clusters of cabbage trees—a giant lily, despite their odd name—encircled knobbly outcroppings of sandstone, worn into a thousand different shapes by the prevailing wind.

"Take lots of pictures," she ordered Esme, backing up a step. "I want to see everything you get up to." Then, as she caught the amused glint in Jerry's eye, she amended, "Almost everything."

As their car sped down the hill, Marjorie waved goodbye, watching them until they were out of sight, then keeping tab for a few minutes more, just in case. With a sigh, she turned back to the café, just in time to see a streak of fluffy grey disappearing around the corner.

"Houdini! You get back right here, this instant." As Marjorie gave chase, she saw Fletcher's startled face press up against the window. With a wave to show his help was welcome, she sprinted down the side of the café, turning the corner to find no trace of the kitten.

"What happened?" Fletcher called out as he reached the opposite side a moment later. "I swear I never touched the door."

"He probably picked the lock on the back door," Marjorie said, only half-joking. "Now, if I were a little troublemaker where would I be?"

"There," Fletcher called, pointing behind Esme's rooms a second before he took off, laughing. "Naughty kitty."

"I don't think you can shame him into coming out of his hiding place," Marjorie said as she caught up to the student, their prey disappearing once again. "More's the pity."

For the next half hour, the café sat neglected while the pair alternated between cries of victory as they spotted the escapee and groans of despair as he eluded their clutches. Finally, just as she thought it might be time to call out the big guns of a bowl full of salmon, Houdini skated too close to Fletcher as he made a run for the corner of Esme's studio.

The young man grabbed hold of the Chartreux's middle and lifted the kitten above his head. "Gotcha!"

"Well done." Marjorie held the first door open for the pair to enter, then made sure the catch snicked back into place before opening the second. A repeat performance would throw her entire schedule off-kilter.

"Look at him," Fletcher said, hands on hips after releasing Houdini. The kitten wandered off to a corner and tossed a feather toy into the air for the pleasure of stalking it until it landed. "He acts like nothing happened."

The poor man sounded out of breath but declined another coffee when Marjorie offered one on the house. Instead, he stared down the hillside at the middle of Hanmer Springs, aghast.

"Why the long face?" she asked, feeling uneasy. "Is something wrong?"

"There are police cars all over the place," Fletcher said, his voice hoarse. All trace of his playful attitude had gone. "It looks like a raid."

Marjorie agreed with his assessment but didn't understand his resulting horror. "It's not your house, is it?"

Fletcher shook his head, but soon made his excuses and departed a good hour earlier than usual.

As she cleared away the table, greeting a new arrival with a cheerful smile and keeping a beady eye out for escaping kittens, Marjorie saw the student had left behind a partially completed clipboard. The required fields were printed in neat handwriting for half the page, then cut off in the middle of a word.

"You scamp," she said to Houdini as she fetched the new customer's order. "If you'd just stayed put for the afternoon, you might've had a new owner."

Monkey Business appeared twice as shocked as Houdini, raising a smile on Marjorie's face.

"I'll just put it safely away here," she said to the kittens, storing the form in the 'odds and sods' drawer under the counter. "Then tomorrow, we'll see if Fletcher picks up again where he left off."

# CHAPTER TWO

The next morning, news of a major drug bust kept Marjorie regaled as she baked up the day's offerings. The police cars Fletcher had seen in the centre of town were just the beginning. Reinforcements had been called in from Christchurch to deal with the numerous arrests and lawyers all over the region fielded calls from suspects.

Given the high quantities of cocaine cited on the radio, Marjorie was surprised their quiet hamlet didn't sport a more overachieving vibe.

"Are you trying to help?" Marjorie asked as

Monkey Business jumped in the air near her feet. "Because if so, you could try measuring out the cinnamon for the pinwheel scones instead of trying to trip me."

At the word cinnamon, his ears perked up, and he padded behind her until she pulled his favourite spice from the rack. With one eye on the clock, she tapped a small cloud of the deliciously scented ingredient into her palm and leant down to let Monkey sniff it. One long inhalation resulted in a furious bout of sneezing. Despite the effect, he always came back for more.

"That's enough," she said, three sneezing fits later. "I need to put these scones in the oven in the next five minutes, otherwise they won't be done in time."

While she washed her hands in the sink, the Persian kitten appeared distinctly unimpressed. With a final sneeze, he trotted over to the sofa and jumped up to survey her from his favourite seat.

"Oh, now you've brought the whole gang out," she said as Chaplin stalked into the kitchen, pouncing on a dropped spoon as though it was prey. Hard on his heels were the Chartreux and a cute black kitten named Midnight. "Everybody out of the kitchen," Marjorie said, clapping her hands. "I've got work to do."

The kittens paid the same amount of attention as always, taking her commands as an invitation to commence mayhem. Luckily, a few toys left on the kitchen windowsill allowed her to entice them into the lounge. Between their squeals and purrs, soon the rest of the posse were waking, ready for a nice hunt.

In different circumstances, that might have involved a dawn stroll giving the early birds a nasty surprise. For Marjorie's kittens, it just meant stumbling their way out of the night playpen and mewing by their empty bowls.

"In a minute," she called out in a sing-song voice. "I just need to pop these into the oven."

With the scones tucked away, Marjorie set the timer for twelve minutes then organised the kittens' breakfast bowls. She'd only just washed her hands again when the oven dinged, announcing the cinnamon treats were ready.

"It's almost a pity to cover this gorgeously cracked brown sugar with icing," she told a curious Chaplin before happily swirling the entire vanilla-flavoured bowl over the top. With the heat of the oven still warming the scone's surface, it melted down to a thin topping, which in time would harden into a shiny glaze.

As she lifted them with practised fingertips onto a wire cooling rack, Marjorie heard the crunch of gravel outside the house. She opened a window, peering down into the carpark below. Nothing.

She'd pulled the window closed when the sound came again. This time, when she poked her head out, Marjorie called, "Is there anybody out there?"

After her experience a few months before, which involved a burglar turned attempted-murderer breaking into the house, Marjorie's nerves weren't up to the task of doing nothing. A horror movie full of ideas floated through her head. Chief amongst them, what would happen to a leading lady if she ventured outside alone.

"Any of you natural born killers want to take a peek outside?" she asked the assembly but received no offers of assistance. "If I call the police and they come down here to investigate nothing, my reputation will be shot."

But better her reputation than her chest.

Marjorie checked her mobile phone was in her pocket before venturing downstairs, flicking on the outside lights for a better view. From the safety of the locked back door, she stared through the rippled glass, squinting to make sense of the view.

A chunky possum ambled into sight, sniffing at everything, whiskers twitching. The thick pelt of winter was shedding now, leaving the animal with large tufts of thick fur moulting to reveal the lighter coat needed for spring and summer.

With a sigh of relief, Marjorie turned the

light back off. She made a mental note to leave a comment on the Department of Conservation site, later. Although the possums appeared cute and cuddly, the introduced species wreaked havoc on local flora and fauna and would displace the natural ecosystem if left unchecked.

"Come on, Kitties," she said at the top of the stairs. "You've only got another hour until showtime so get your sparkle on!"

"FINALLY!" Cecelia exclaimed when she walked into the café. "I get my favourite spot."

She put her purse down on the table, beaming a smile at Marjorie as she walked over to the counter. "Did the student sleep in?"

"I'm not sure, he hasn't popped in yet. Do you want your usual?"

Cecelia nodded, giving an exultant laugh as Chaplin and Houdini rushed over to see how she was doing. "I see being early has its advantages."

Marjorie checked the clock, feeling a tad disquieted that Fletcher hadn't turned up that morning. He'd been such a habitual customer, she had to push down the expectation he should have called to say he wasn't coming.

Ridiculous. Her clientele could take a day off without checking in!

"Here you go," she said, carrying across Cecelia's order. "Do you want me to shoo them away a bit?"

In the short timeframe she'd been there, half the kittens in the café had crowded around the woman's table, butting against her ankles and mewing.

"No, they're fine." Cecelia leant over to stroke Chaplin before spraying on hand sanitiser. "What a treat to have all their attention to myself."

"Well, let me know. I think there's something odd in the air today because they're overly clingy."

Already that morning, Marjorie had freed

an elderly woman who'd been trapped in a corner by half a dozen kittens, running at her feet when she tried to leave. Usually, they saved the dawdling around the legs performance for her alone, but this morning they were sharing the love.

Near ten o'clock, Regina Ashford dropped by the café for a quick cup of coffee. "It looks like your department has its work cut out for it," Marjorie commented as she prepared a cappuccino with extra chocolate on the side. "Is this the largest drug bust you've ever worked?"

Regina snorted, shaking her head. "Not likely. As soon as Sergeant Matthewson called the other regions in for extra help, we lost control of the case." She took a sip of her coffee, leaving a foam moustache on her upper lip. "This morning, I've been out on my usual beat as though nothing exciting's happening at all."

"How dare they?" Marjorie set up a second cup without being asked. "Just because they're more heavily resourced doesn't mean they know the job any better. You're the one with the local knowledge."

"To be fair," Regina said with a shrug, "I haven't been back in town long enough to qualify as an entrenched local. People are just as likely to talk to one of the Christchurch cops as they are to me."

"Don't sell yourself short. There're plenty of folks in town who remember you from your first stint here."

Regina raised her eyebrows, apparently unconvinced. "Hm. Well, it's nice of you to say, anyway. Have you had any trouble up here lately?"

"We had a kitten escape yesterday. Apart from that, nope."

The officer soon took her leave and Marjorie spent the rest of the day alternating between serving and checking her watch. She'd grown used to chatting with Fletcher during the lulls between busy stretches and readied an amusing titbit only to have no one but the kittens to tell.

"Still, at least you won't scold me when I

go too far," she said to Monkey Business, who promptly jumped a foot in the air, twisting in mid-air to scamper away. "Or you might," Marjorie amended with a giggle.

THE NEXT DAY, Fletcher was a no-show again. The day following that, Saturday, was busy as usual, with little time for Marjorie to stop and lament his absence. Still, it worried her when she checked the form on the clipboard.

The half-completed details were a chance for Houdini to find a new home. As she opened the cupboard under the stairs to pull out the vacuum cleaner and found herself with a faceful of Chartreux kitten instead, Marjorie realised his adoption would give her poor heart a rest from unexpected shocks, too.

Sunday was her half-day, which wasn't entirely accurate considering her closing time only moved from three to one o'clock. Still, with no sign of her resident student again,

Marjorie decided it was time to take matters into her own hands.

The fifteen dollars a day wouldn't make or break her but the loss of an adoptive parent and friend was a harder cross to bear.

Since Fletcher had so kindly filled out his address on the adoption form, Marjorie closed up the café right on the dot so she could turn up on his doorstep and find out for herself if her worries were valid.

# CHAPTER THREE

When Marjorie turned up at the address, she did a double-take. Her expectation for student housing was poor, cheap, and nasty—not necessarily in that order. Instead, Fletcher's home was a tidy, three-bedroom structure made from sturdy brick, with a neatly clipped front lawn and weed-free flowerbeds.

By the time she reached the front door, she'd decided he must rent a room or board with the true owners. When she pressed the doorbell, Marjorie waited for a middle-aged man or woman to open the door.

Nobody answered.

After a few tries, giving far longer than anybody needed even if she'd caught them mid-shower, Marjorie walked to the side of the house and peered along the edge of the property.

A gate separated the back yard from the driveway. It was possible someone could be out there and not hear the doorbell.

"It's not trespassing until you open something you shouldn't, or someone tells you to leave," she whispered in reassurance while striding along the driveway. The garage door was wide open with no vehicle parked inside the space. Surely that meant the owners were nearby.

Hanmer Springs might be a town where you could forget about locking your doors but leaving a treasure trove of tools on display in an open garage was another matter altogether.

"Hello. Anybody there?" she called out at the end of the drive. "I'm looking for Fletcher."

A crash from the next-door neighbour's yard made Marjorie jump, then a tousled head of hair stuck up over the fence. "Argh," a voice announced as another crash sounded. "Don't worry, I'm alright."

"Good to know," Marjorie called out, suppressing a burst of laughter. "Can I help you?"

"Just give me a second." This time when the tousled hair turned up it was high enough up to display a face beneath. A grinning man with rough skin and patches of deep crimson on the nose and cheeks, like he'd spent a lifetime on the rough seas or with a whisky bottle clutched in his hand. His blond hair stood up at all angles. "You're after Fletcher?"

"Yes, that's right." Marjorie wandered over to the rickety wooden fence, holding her hand up to shake. "I'm Marjorie Hardaway. Fletcher usually comes into my café for at least five or six hours a day, but I haven't seen him since Wednesday."

"He took off late Wednesday afternoon," the

man said, pushing a lock of hair out of his eyes. "I'm Efron Jackson." He reached over, touching the tips of Marjorie's fingers for a second before he jerked backwards, another crash sounding.

"How about I come over?" she shouted, trying desperately hard not to giggle. "It'll be easier."

She didn't wait for an answer, just hurrying along the driveway and up the opposite path. Efron was struggling to free himself from an old council recycling bin, the sturdy plastic construction not equal to his weight.

"Let me help you," Marjorie said, rushing forward before the man toppled over again. "Is anything broken?"

"Just this bin and my pride," Efron said with such an easy grin, she felt certain his pride had survived unscathed. "Now, where were we?"

"Fletcher leaving on Wednesday."

"Ah," he tipped his head back, rubbing the side of his nose. "That's right. The lad's usually up for a chat and a cuppa but he seemed in an awful hurry."

"Oh, dear," Marjorie said, pointing to Efron's leg. "You're bleeding."

The man's face turned white as chalk and he sagged.

"Lean against me," she said, rushing in to catch him before he fell. A friend in primary school, Alice, had been prone to faint at the sight of blood and this many years later, Marjorie still recognised the warning signs.

"I'll get the blood on you."

"In which case, it'll wash off. Is your door unlocked?"

When Efron didn't answer, Marjorie headed there, anyway. The man wasn't much taller than her, but she couldn't support his weight for long. Especially not if he lost consciousness altogether.

With a 'thank goodness' under her breath, she discovered the door not only unlocked but also off the latch. She tipped her shoulder against it, dragging Efron over the step and depositing him onto a chair in the kitchen.

"Where are your first aid supplies and I'll get this sorted," she said, wrapping a tea towel around the man's lower leg to stem the blood flow in the meantime.

"Bathroom."

"Which is?" As Efron sagged, Marjorie propped him up with one hand, snapping her fingers under his nose. "Don't do that. Bite down on your tongue or something. If you slump onto the floor, you'll be staying there until bigger help than me arrives."

He shook himself, eyelids fluttering before he straightened slightly. "Down the hallway, second on the right. There should be something in the cabinet."

Marjorie pulled out everything relevant and dumped it on the kitchen floor. While Efron stared at the lighting fixtures, she cleaned out the wound, plucked a shard of plastic from his calf, and taped it up with a plentiful supply of sticking plasters.

"There you go," she said, groaning as she stood. "You can look now."

Efron offered her an embarrassed shrug.

"Sorry about that. I've always had a problem with the sight of"—he waved his hand—"you know, but the Lord blessed me with being clumsy, as well. It's a powerful mix."

This time, Marjorie couldn't hold back the giggles. "I'm so sorry," she said between splutters. "I'm not laughing at your injured leg."

"Don't worry." Efron stood, flexing out his injury and tipping her a wink. "As long as you're my nursemaid, you get to laugh all you want. Cup of tea?"

"That'll be lovely."

She sat and watched him work, half forgetting the reason she was there at all until a steaming cup was firmly in her hand.

"Has Fletcher lived next door to you for long?"

Efron sat back, patting his tummy. He reminded her of a long-gone kitten named Humphrey who'd loved to loll about on his back, patting his fluffy belly. If anyone else tried to do the same, the claws would come out.

"I don't keep great track of dates. The curse of being self-employed and without many cares in the world." He screwed up his face in concentration. "Maybe a month or two. No longer than that." Efron waited for a beat, then smiled. "Probably."

"And what about flatmates? With the rental on a nice place like that, I guess he has a few others living with him."

"Oh, no. None that I've seen. Just Fletcher on his lonesome. That's why I never feel bad about checking if he wants to join me in a beer while watching a game. When a man's on his own, you need to watch out he doesn't get lonely, you know?"

"I'm sure he appreciates it," Marjorie said. "That's why he told me he spends most of his days in my café. Doing coursework via distance learning is fine for an education but he misses the company he'd get at university."

"I can see that." Efron ran a hand through his hair again, showing why it was so messy. "He has a girlfriend, I think. And an older fellow stops by regularly."

Marjorie had never seen Fletcher with a woman, but she nodded at the reference to an older man. "Is he the one dressed up in a checked jacket with leather elbows?"

"That's the one."

A week or more ago, Marjorie had bumped into Fletcher and a companion while out shopping. The fellow with him had introduced himself as a professor of philosophy—the young man's subject—but Fletcher had pulled him away before they could exchange more than simple pleasantries. She'd guessed he was embarrassed, much the same way she would have been as a child, caught talking with a teacher outside of school.

"What's his girlfriend's name?"

The man shrugged. "Never spent any time on the subject. She drives a red car if that helps."

Marjorie screwed up her nose, giving a small laugh. "I'm sure that narrows it down."

"To the most popular colour on the road, yep."

With the information about Fletcher drying up, Marjorie made her excuses to leave. "If I take a closer look through the windows, promise you won't phone the police?"

He gave her a Scout's salute.

The front windows revealed nothing of interest but in the rear, through the window just by the backyard fence, she saw a stack of boxes piled high. With judicious use of squinting, Marjorie could make out they were laptop computers, at least if the outside of the boxes was to be believed.

"How on earth can he afford any of this?" she mused to herself.

"And what business is that of yours?" a furious female voice asked. "This is private property and if you don't have the authorisation to be here, I suggest you leave."

# CHAPTER FOUR

"I'm so sorry," Marjorie said, blushing until she felt like a hot flush had her in its clutches. "You must be Fletcher's girlfriend. I was just trying to find out if he's okay."

"And who are you?" The blonde woman perched her hands on her hips, glaring through blue eyes as sharp as icicles. She gave Marjorie a quick glance up and down, her expression turning scornful. "His mum?"

*If I was, you'd regret saying it in that tone, young lady!*

Marjorie clamped down on the thought,

not wanting to antagonise the situation any further. Instead, she introduced herself, adding, "I run the kitten café just up the hill."

"That place." The young blonde shook her head. "Fletcher spends more time in there than's good for him."

Since the claim held a lot of truth, Marjorie didn't defend it. She nodded along, trying a smile on for size. "Do you know where he's run off to? He left in quite a hurry the other day and I haven't seen him since."

The young woman lifted her nose in the air. "I don't see how his whereabouts are your concern. Unless he ran out without paying a tab, then I think you should respect his privacy."

"Oh, of course." Marjorie took a step back, feeling small and old and stupid. If it hadn't been for the glint of tears in the blonde's eyes, she would have cut and run right then. "It's just I got worried. Silly, really." She paused for a second, trying not to stare as a tear ran down the woman's face. "I'm sorry but I didn't catch your name."

"It's Adelaide," the young lady said. "Adelaide Rowland."

"Well, I'm pleased to meet you, Adelaide. Fletcher mentions you all the time." Marjorie kept her fingers crossed as she spoke the lie, content with the deceit because the young man *should* talk about his girlfriend.

Adelaide's sniffles came farther apart and as she plunged her hands into her jeans' pocket, Marjorie fished a travel pack of tissues out of her purse.

"Are you crying because Fletcher's done something awful or because you're worried about him, too?"

The young woman took a deep breath and blew her nose. "I don't know where he's got to. On Tuesday he was all over my DMs, then he just seemed to disappear."

"Efron next door"—Marjorie jerked her head in explanation—"says he took off on Wednesday afternoon and hasn't been back since. Is he usually in touch with you during the week?"

"Yeah, off and on. He doesn't like to visit

my place because I've got four roommates and they never seem to leave the house, but he often invites me over here or we chat online."

"Do you have a phone number for him?"

Adelaide nodded, her eyes welling up again. "I've been texting him non-stop. Not desperate-like but enough to prompt him to send a reply." She shook her head, a lone tear streaking down the side of her face. "So far, nothing."

"Is he the type to let his phone run out of battery?"

The young woman gave a curt laugh. "Not likely. He's attached to that thing worse than I am with mine. Sometimes we'll be sat next to each other on the couch and he won't drag his eyes off the screen."

From where Marjorie stood, that could apply to anyone at all, nowadays, but she kept her lip buttoned and nodded for Adelaide to continue.

"Even if he broke the thing, he'd be into the shop the next day as soon as they opened, getting a new one. It's not like him to be out of touch at all, and with everything that's been going on around here..." She trailed off into a sob.

Marjorie waited for a minute but when Adelaide didn't resume, she prompted, "What sorts of things have been going on?"

"With the police raiding everyone in sight." The young woman gave her a stare full of curiosity. "Haven't you heard about it on Facebook? There're people being dragged into the station left, right, and centre."

"You mean the drug raids?" Marjorie said, hoping she'd got the wrong end of the stick. But the blonde nodded. "Surely, Fletcher's not caught up with drugs."

"The police aren't stopping there. Half my friends have been in the station this week, being asked questions like invading everyone's privacy is perfectly okay."

If they were breaking the law, then it was okay in Marjorie's book, but again she held her tongue. The thought of the boxes of laptops in the rear room weighed on her mind. Perhaps she would have been better off sticking to her kittens and her café and leaving Fletcher to worry about himself.

"He'd never do drugs," Adelaide said in a firm voice. "Fletcher's too fixated on getting his degree that he'd never risk it all on something as stupid as that."

"I'm glad to hear it." Marjorie pinched the bridge of her nose, squeezing her eyes shut. With the new information pouring out of this unexpected source, she wasn't sure what the next best step was.

"We should go to the police," she decided aloud, glancing at Adelaide and feeling relief the younger woman was nodding. "First off, if they've been questioning everyone as you say, they might know where he's hiding out. Second, if they haven't heard from him either, I'd say it's time we report Fletcher missing."

"Missing?"

Marjorie gave a firm nod. "It's the right thing to do. Unless you know how to contact Fletcher's family?"

Adelaide shook her head glumly. "I'm not even sure he has any."

Marjorie tried not to compare the young couple's relationship with her own fledgling romance with Braden. By the end of the first week, they not only knew about their family members but had their life stories and favourite anecdotes down pat.

"Come on," she said, touching the back of Adelaide's elbow to propel her forward. "Your car or mine?"

MARJORIE HADN'T SEEN the constable standing behind the police station counter before. It gave her second thoughts until she remembered Regina's complaint about the 'foreigners' taking over.

"Hey," she said with a forced smile. "I'd like to report a missing person."

"Who's that then?" the man asked, and she bent forward to read his name tag. Sutton.

"It's a friend of mine, Fletcher Byrne. Nobody's seen him since Wednesday."

PC Sutton turned to his computer, typing

in something and staring hard at the screen. "Family?"

"You mean Fletcher's family?" Marjorie qualified, then shook her head when Sutton nodded. "I don't know."

"Close then, were you?"

Regina walked into the office through a side door and read the situation in about three-quarters of a second. "Why don't you do the prisoner checks?" she suggested, moving up to the counter. "And I'll handle this complaint."

"It's not a complaint," Sutton said.

"Not yet," Regina countered, shoving herself into position so the officer had no choice but to leave.

"Thanks for that," Marjorie said, feeling a flush of gratitude for her old friend. "I don't think he's enjoying his time here."

"Yeah, he's got a few troubles on his mind," Regina said with a wink. "None of which I could tell a layperson, such as speaking out of turn during an interview and being demoted to office duties until he relearns his place."

Marjorie laughed, then stopped when she turned to beckon Adelaide forward. "This is Fletcher's girlfriend, and she hasn't seen him either. We're both worried."

"Well, follow me and we'll go into a quiet room where you can gather your thoughts. I think there's an interview room spare. We've quietened down again finally."

They followed Regina through a short corridor and into a windowless room. The air conditioning unit made a ticking sound, like it was counting down the time to a complete breakdown. Still, it was nicer than standing at the front desk where anybody might wander past.

"Now, what was your name again?" Regina asked Adelaide, using a manual form instead of the computer. "Can you spell it?"

When she'd written their details, the officer got back to Fletcher's family again. "If you don't know, it's okay, but didn't he ever mention anybody to you?"

Marjorie shook her head, aware of how

shallow their conversations had been. Adelaide frowned at the table, pressing a finger hard against the veneer until the tip turned white.

"A brother?" she finally said, as though asking a question. "I think Fletcher might've mentioned how his parents always liked his brother better."

"And his parents are still alive?"

"I guess."

"What'd he do?"

"He's a student," Marjorie said when Adelaide fell silent. "Fletcher's completing a degree through a distance learning program at the university."

"Massey," Adelaide said, stirring into action again. "He's studying Philosophy." She gave a small snort. "He said he's studying hard to make sure when he graduates, he'll be unemployable in his chosen field."

Regina laughed and nodded, scribbling a few more notes. Adelaide gave her information about Fletcher's social network accounts and phone numbers while Marjorie handed across her phone, which had a recent photograph of him playing with Houdini.

"We've got enough to follow up on," Regina said as they came to a close, "but if there's anything else you think of, let me know. Every bit of information, no matter how small, can help in these cases."

"What will happen now?" Adelaide asked, picking at her fingernails. "Should we wait here?"

"You go home, and we'll make inquiries."

"Most people turn up safe and sound, don't they?" Marjorie asked, hoping to reassure the nervous young woman beside her.

"Many do but until I get started, we won't know anything." Regina got half up from her seat, then sat down again. "I must warn you that if we find Fletcher and he's safe and sound, that's the end for us."

"What do you mean?" Adelaide asked in a breathy whisper.

"I mean, he's an adult and if he doesn't want to be in contact with either of you again, we can't make him. It may not be the case," she said, raising a palm to stop Adelaide's protestations, "but it's a possibility."

"That's fine." Marjorie stood up and nudged the woman's shoulder until she did too. "Our main priority is to make sure he's safe. Once we both know that, he can do what he likes."

Adelaide looked like she wanted to protest against the statement, but Marjorie pulled her out of the station before she could say anything, mouthing a *thank you* at Regina over her shoulder.

## CHAPTER FIVE

After seeing Adelaide home, Marjorie dropped by Braden's place to check if he was in the mood for company. Although they'd now seen each other socially for a month or more, their relationship hadn't progressed.

Sometimes, Marjorie wanted to grab the man by the lapels and press her lips against his, in case he didn't know that was what she wanted. Other times, it felt better and more companionable just to keep the status quo.

"Do you want to go for a walk?" he asked once her knocking cajoled him away from a computer game. His hair was flattened in a crease on top of his head where headphones had been sitting, possibly for hours.

"I'd like to check on my kittens first," she said, walking arm in arm to her car. "But there's a nice forest trail just up the road from the café if you like."

On the drive, she filled him in on her day and he seemed genuinely concerned for Fletcher's wellbeing. It made her feel much better. Every minute that passed since going to the station had increased the sense she'd overreacted.

"It's a long time to go AWOL," Braden agreed. "Especially if it looks like he was coming straight home."

"Do you know him at all?" It occurred to Marjorie that someone with a stash of laptops in their front room might operate in the same circles as a computer engineer.

But Braden put her right on that score. "Never been a customer of mine. Given his age, he's probably a dab hand at everything it took me years of training to learn."

When Marjorie walked inside the café, a disturbing silence greeted her. With her pulse increasing, she lunged upstairs, expecting signs of a catastrophe. Instead, the kittens were all inside the playpen, fast asleep.

All but Houdini.

"Where've you got to, you rascal?" she murmured, quickly scanning each room and coming up empty. "I swear, that kitten will be the death of me."

"Heart attacks from fear are a lot less common than you seem to think," Braden said, joining in the hunt with a smile. "Otherwise, surprise parties would be banned as instruments of death."

"They should be," Marjorie said darkly, remembering one birthday close to the end of her marriage. She'd come home from a long day at her then job of office manager, only to have all her husband's friends jump out at her from the shadows. They'd expected her to be pleased with another five hours of what appeared to her to be nothing but hard work.

If he'd invited her friends, it might have

been different. The fact he didn't know them just proved their separation was long overdue.

"Would this be the kitten you're looking for?" Braden asked, pointing to a gap between the fridge and the bench from which a pair of golden eyes stared back. "I'm not sure how to get him out."

"That's fine," Marjorie said. "I don't think he's stuck—the wily thing probably couldn't get wedged in if he tried. I'm happy knowing he hasn't got out again."

With her mind at rest, they set off up the hill for the start of the trail. The forest around Hanmer Springs was lined with different walking tracks for all stages of fitness.

Braden cast a concerned glance at the entrance marker. "That looks like it's a few levels above my sedentary lifestyle."

Marjorie hooked her arm through his elbow. "You're the one who suggested a walk. It's too late to back out now."

Despite his misgivings, soon Braden took the lead as the path narrowed. The rich earth beneath their feet was soft with fallen pine needles and the songs of native birds rang out from the tree branches, keeping them company.

"My only misgiving with heading downhill," Braden said a good half hour later, "is that at some point, I'll be expected to go uphill again."

"If you get too stuck, I'll walk back alone and come back with a car for you."

"What an insult to my manliness."

Although she laughed, Marjorie felt increasingly uneasy as they ventured farther into the woods. Usually, she'd love the chance for a good hike but with her mind on other matters, the deep shadows of the closing forest lowered her mood.

"Look at this," Braden said, pulling on a pink ribbon tied around a bridge strut. Considering the creek it traversed was barely more than a trickle, it seemed more like stage dressing than a necessity, even for the most unskilled walker.

"There's another one over there," Marjorie said, pointing. In fact, there were quite a few dotted around the place. Until Braden drew her attention to them, they'd simply appeared as part of the colourful forest.

"If they're marking out a trail, I hate to think of the poor saps who follow it," Braden said, fishing a large rock out of the muddy creek bed with another pink ribbon tied around it. "What are they expecting people to do with this one? Step in the middle of the mud?"

"Like you," Marjorie said with a laugh, seeing the bottom half of Braden's jeans were now coated with the stuff. "I think you'll need to give them a good wash."

He tried to make it up the short slope back onto the trail but gave a surprised chuckle when he couldn't. "The mud's sucking onto my shoes," he said, bending over with laughter as he exerted more effort, only to end up in the same situation. "Can you give me a hand?"

"Only if you don't pull me... Oh!" Too late, Marjorie felt her balance tip as she slid down the incline. Soon she too was doubling over with tears streaming down her face. "Why's… this… so… funny?" she said between bouts.

"I give up," Braden said, throwing his arms out to either side in dramatic fashion. "We'll just have to stay here forever. King and Queen of the muddiest stream in the country."

"Stream is an overstretch for what this is," Marjorie said, snorting as she gained one foothold only to slide back down again.

"Careful. If you upset the river, it'll take its revenge!"

As Marjorie tried to turn and remonstrate, she overbalanced, one hand squeezing deep into the mud. "Ugh," she uttered as the cold slime oozed between her fingers. "Help. We need help!"

"Who're you yelling to? I'm already helping."

Marjorie was consumed in another burst of laughter, then steeled the muscles in her thighs to wrench her hand out of the mud. With the sudden momentum of freedom, she came close to toppling in the other direction, but Braden steadied her.

"I think we're stuck here forever," he whispered, his eyes twinkling with mischief. "To think I used to laugh at all my eighties heroes getting stuck in quicksand. I should've shown more respect."

"We could die," Marjorie said with wide eyes, her solemnity only ruined when she dissolved into giggles again. "They'll find our bones years from now and be left wondering what happened."

"Do you think..." Braden stopped, leaning in closer to whisper in Marjorie's ear. "Do you think the pink ribbons were there to warn us?"

His soft breath against her ear sent a delicious shiver running down her spine. "If so, I'd count that as a massive fail."

Braden took hold of Marjorie's chin, tilting her head back. She closed her eyes as he leaned in, relishing the warm press of his lips against hers.

"Get a room, Grandpa!"

The hooting call of a cycling teenager broke the spell. Braden turned and lunged for the path, grabbing hold of an overhead tree branch as his feet came close to slipping away. Once he had a solid footing, he turned and grasped hold of Marjorie's arm, pulling her free.

"Well," she said, bending to wipe her muddy hand on the dropped pine needles. "That was an unexpected adventure."

Braden grinned at her with a delighted expression that warmed a fire in her belly. "Yes, we should try it again sometime."

NEITHER OF THEM was in the mood for more walking so they cut through the woods at an angle, ending up on the side of the road. From there, it was a quick walk up the hill, back to the café. As Marjorie wiped her hair back from her forehead, Braden wrinkled his nose. "I think you might need to wash that hand before it causes any more trouble."

After letting them inside and checking in the bathroom mirror, she saw a giant streak of mud across her forehead. "It's probably good for wrinkles," she assured her reflection as she scrubbed it away, then poked out her tongue. The red highlights in her cheeks had nothing to do with the energetic walk or the dirt.

Although she would've enjoyed it more if Braden stayed, he excused himself a few minutes later, citing his online gaming companions as an excuse. Marjorie tried not to mind, feeding the kittens and making a quick sandwich for her own dinner.

When Houdini jumped out at Marjorie from atop the kitchen cupboards, she flicked him with water, then smiled. "I'd better not drive you away. At the rate my relationship's progressing, Braden will probably ask me to move in with him a week after we're both dead."

Houdini blinked his large golden eyes, then trotted over to the sofa, disappearing in behind it.

"Thanks. I didn't want to spend time with you, either." Monkey Business gave a start and backed up three steps. "Not you, honey. I was talking to another cat. Do you want to keep me company while I watch TV and wallow?"

The answer to that was a firm yes and Marjorie drifted off to sleep on the sofa. When she woke, the moonlight was streaming in through the window, so bright it lit up the whole room with silver tones.

She crossed to the window, watching the play of light as the clouds floated across the face of the moon. It cast shadows across Esme's massage studio, fooling her into thinking there was something in there, moving.

"I'm being daft, aren't I?" she asked Monkey as he batted his nose into the backs of her legs. "Better get to bed otherwise it'll be morning before I know it."

She turned off the blank television and yawned all the way to the bedroom. The next morning, the urge to thump off the alarm was stronger than usual, and only a chocolate Persian paw in her face convinced Marjorie not to hit the snooze button.

By the time she opened the café, the coffee

machine had already been warmed up by preparing two Americanos. Marjorie was considering a third when the door opened, and Fletcher walked inside the cafe.

"Are you the manager?" he asked, crossing to the counter with a grim expression on his face. "I need to speak to someone named Marjorie Hardaway."

# CHAPTER SIX

*I*t only took Marjorie a few seconds to scan his face and recognise the small differences. Fletcher's ears stuck out farther than this man's. His eyes were more almond-shaped and his nose turned down at the tip rather than up.

"I'm Marjorie," she said after regaining the power of speech. "And you must be Fletcher's brother."

"Duncan," he said, shaking her hand. "I'm his twin."

"Yeah, I got that," she said with a laugh. "I

couldn't work out why he was acting like he didn't know me!"

"Are you good friends?"

"Not really. He comes in here most days though, and stays for hours, so we chat quite a lot."

Duncan pulled a phone out of his pocket, scrolling through a few screens before showing her a picture. It was the same one she'd passed to the police. Fletcher playing with Houdini, looking like he didn't have a care in the world. "Did you take this photo?"

"Yeah."

Houdini scampered down the stairs, nearly toppling over in his excitement to reach Duncan. He placed a paw on the man's calf, patting it repeatedly when he didn't look down straight away.

"That's the co-star from the picture," Marjorie said, nodding to the kitten. "Fletcher formed quite an attachment to him." She pulled out the clipboard from under the counter. "He left this on the table the last day I saw him. Got halfway through the questions, then sprinted out of here as though his feet were on fire."

Duncan bent down and moved Houdini away from his leg, giving his butt a little shove to guide him away. "Fletcher always had a soft spot for cats," he said in a tone communicating he didn't share the same feature.

"He seemed to enjoy it here, that's for sure." Marjorie frowned at a thought. "Did the police tell you I was the one to report him missing?"

"No." He held out the phone again, pointing to Esme's blurry massage sign in the background. "But it didn't take me long to work out where this had been taken."

"You should be a detective."

He wrinkled his nose, turning and staring around the room before facing her again. "Why'd you report him if you barely knew him?"

"I didn't say *that*. For a customer, I knew him very well."

Duncan shrugged. "It just seems odd. Where did he sit? Did he have a favourite table?"

"Over there," Marjorie said, pointing. "Why don't you take a seat, and I'll bring you over something to eat and a cup of coffee."

He sat, accepting her offer with such haste Marjorie had to suppress a smile as she turned to her workstation. With a plate full up with two cinnamon rolls and a pat of butter, she balanced another Americano for herself and a fluffy cappuccino for Duncan and walked to the table.

"Thanks for this," he said. "I spend a sleepless night, convincing myself I should let the police handle things and just go to work as usual." He took a quick sip, testing the temperature, then a longer one. "As you can see, I didn't make a persuasive argument."

"What more can I help you with?" Marjorie sipped at her coffee slowly, aware her nerves were already hyper. "I wasn't able to tell the police very much, I'm afraid."

"I don't know." Duncan rubbed his hands

over his face. "How about friends? Do you know who he hung around with?"

"His girlfriend's Adelaide Rowland. She lives down in the township if you want her address."

"That'll be good." He sat back, staring over her shoulder, out the window. "Although I suppose it's early to be making house calls."

"Oh, dang it!"

Marjorie turned at the sharp voice to see Cecelia standing in the entrance. "I'm too late again, I see."

"Too late for what?" Duncan asked, his eyebrows arching.

Cecelia frowned, glancing from him to Marjorie with a query in her eyes. "To sit at my favourite table."

"This is Duncan Byrne," Marjorie said, getting to her feet and picking up the empty dishes. "He's Fletcher's brother. And this is Cecelia Armock, another regular at the café."

"I can move," Duncan offered as Marjorie retreated behind the counter. "It's no bother. Did you know Fletcher well?"

As the two of them chatted, Cecelia softening more than Marjorie had witnessed before, she picked up with the morning tasks she'd dropped to serve the unexpected arrival. Houdini decided it was a great time to play, nudging her in the legs and depositing a feather toy at her feet.

"Why don't you take it over to the table?" she whispered to the kitten, pointing to where Duncan and Cecelia were deep in conversation. "I'm sure they'd appreciate the gesture."

But the grey kitten just stared at her through his golden eyes, playing statue. Marjorie gave a sigh and fluttered the feather just out of the Chartreux's reach, keeping him busy chasing it until more morning customers arrived.

"I will take that address if you have it," Duncan said an hour later as he came up to the counter. "Once I've been back to the police station to check in with them, I'll pay her a visit. It'll be a decent hour by then."

Thinking of Braden's late waking habits,

Marjorie warned, "Leave it until after lunchtime, just to be sure."

"Perhaps you're right. Do you know of a good place to stay in town? Not too expensive."

"Aren't you staying at your brother's house?"

Duncan shrugged. "It feels like an intrusion to stay there without his permission."

"But he'd ask you to stay with him if he were here, wouldn't he?"

"I suppose."

"And you might find something useful inside." Marjorie clapped a hand to her forehead. "Except you don't have a key. Doh. Forget I spoke."

"Actually"—Duncan fished around in his inside jacket pocket and pulled out a house key—"I do. We exchanged them the last time I was up here."

"Isn't that inconvenient if you're both renting?"

Another shrug. "It's a three-hour round trip, and I'd get to see my brother. Hardly the worst arrangement in the world." His face clouded over. "I'd feel funny going in his space alone."

"Do you want me to come with you?" Marjorie put forward the offer with little thought and was glad to see the man's countenance brighten. "I can't come now"— she waved her hands towards the few diners —"but come back at three and we can go together."

The rest of her Monday opening hours passed so quickly, Marjorie felt she'd only had time to blink and Duncan was back in the café. Houdini trotted up to see him, sniffing at the man's foot and backing away with a few forlorn mews.

"I guess I don't measure up to my brother, eh?" Duncan asked as he leaned down to give the upset kitten a pat. Houdini allowed a few strokes, then trotted away. A moment later, he jumped up on the windowsill, attempting to push Chaplin from his favourite sunning spot. The ragdoll bristled and held firm. Eventually, the two settled down together.

"Are they okay on their own?" Duncan asked as Marjorie popped away the café sign and locked the entrance behind her.

"They'll be fine," she reassured him. "When I'm out, Monkey Business is in charge and he lets them all know it. Sometimes I think they prefer having a rest from human interaction. Are you happy giving me a lift or would you prefer us to take separate vehicles?"

"Jump in mine. I don't have a problem dropping you home later."

As they travelled down the hillside, Marjorie pointed out a few spots of local interest. The turnoff to the campsite was one, along with the lovely walking trails surrounding the Dog Stream Reserve.

She regaled him with a quick anecdote about finding a mushroom there that—by the time she found a matching description online to verify its safety to eat—had decomposed into a mess of brown liquid and cream spores.

"It's the next turnoff on the right," Marjorie instructed as they drew closer to Fletcher's home. "And then the third house on the right, with the cream gate."

They pulled up outside, and she waved to Efron whose tousled head was just visible over the sectional fence.

"Did you know the police have been around?" he called out as soon as she slid from the passenger seat. "Yesterday, I kept telling myself everything was okay, then this morning, the old blues and twos were pulling up outside my door."

"I hope they didn't cause you any trouble," Marjorie said, walking right up to the fence as Efron briefly ducked out of sight, then banged his head straightening up again. "Adelaide and I decided we should let them know, just in case."

"Hm. Well, they got nothing out of me, I can tell you. I'm not a grass."

Marjorie frowned. "Fletcher isn't in any trouble. They're just trying to find him so we can make sure he's okay."

Efron tapped the side of his nose. "My lips are sealed."

Giving up, she walked over to join Duncan at the front door. His hand shook as he tried to slot the key home. "I'm terrified we're going to walk inside and there'll be this awful smell."

"Oh, don't." Marjorie gently elbowed him to one side. "I'll take a sniff and let you know if it's all clear but I'm sure Fletcher isn't hiding away inside here. His car's nowhere around."

Still, her heart beat at a rapid pace as she pulled the door open and took a tentative step inside the room. Apart from the slight mustiness of an unaired house, there was nothing to assault her olfactory senses.

"Come on in," she said with a nod to Duncan. "If your brother is hiding away inside here, he's still alive and well."

Duncan scowled. "If he is skulking around in here, he won't stay that way for long."

But inside, there was no sign of Fletcher. At first, the two stayed together as they searched the kitchen and the front parlour, separating as they walked down the corridor and popped their heads in the side rooms.

"What is all this stuff?" Marjorie asked, seeing the boxes of computer equipment from the other side. The unopened boxes were stacked high in the bedroom, cutting out the afternoon sunlight from the side window.

"I don't know." Duncan frowned as he checked the labels, then lifted a box and hefted its weight. "Do you have a pocketknife handy?"

"Do I look like a woman who carries weapons?" Marjorie asked with a smile, rather fancying the idea. "I'll see if there's something suitable in the kitchen.

She strode back along the corridor, picking up a pair of scissors from the knife block. As she stepped out of the room, movement from the adjoining property caught her eye and she walked into the lounge instead.

Efron stood with a pair of binoculars fixed

on the room where Duncan was, and the boxes of equipment. When Marjorie crossed to the window and pulled aside the net curtain, his focus changed, then he ducked behind the fence.

"I'm just popping next door, okay?" Marjorie said as she handed over the scissors. "There's something weird going on with Fletcher's neighbour."

"Need a hand?"

Marjorie hesitated for a second before shaking her head. "Nah, I'm good. There's plenty of foot traffic to yell to if I get caught off guard."

Besides, she couldn't imagine the rumpled and slightly disorientated man of the day before posing a threat. One push and his natural clumsiness would take care of the rest.

Efron was coming out the front door as Marjorie hurried up the path and he staggered to one side to avoid a collision. "Why were you peering at Fletcher's house?" Marjorie demanded before the man could open his mouth. "I saw you with your binoculars."

"I was… bird-watching," Efron said with a sickly grin. "Nothing more. You've misunderstood—"

"I understand exactly what I saw." Marjorie inched closer to the man until she invaded his personal space. "Do you have something illegal going on with Fletcher? Is that why you were so desperate to avoid talking to the police?"

"I don't know what you're on about," Efron said with an indignant sniff. "I'm just a next-door neighbour who occasionally likes to share a beer. Nothing more."

"So you won't mind if we call the police and ask them about the stash of boxes in Fletcher's room?"

Efron's face drained of blood, his lips so pale they appeared blue. "Now, now. There's no need to trouble our boys in—"

"My friend is an officer. I swear, it's no trouble on my part." Marjorie hauled her phone out of her pocket and clicked into her contacts list. "Her private number is listed right here."

"No!" Efron struck the phone from her hand and it skittered across the concrete path, landing in the grass. "It's nothing to do with his disappearance, okay? Why don't you leave well enough alone?"

# CHAPTER SEVEN

*T*he phone screen was dirty but not scratched and once Marjorie gave it a swipe with her sleeve, it appeared as good as new. She'd assured Efron that she wouldn't bring his stash of goods to the police's attention if he told her everything about the operation.

Despite his initial floundering, he soon cooperated, once Duncan came across to see what was holding Marjorie up, that was.

"He just stores things for me," Efron explained, holding a mug of tea between his hands like he needed the warmth despite the late spring day. "Stuff falls off the back of a truck and it needs to hide away somewhere until the drivers forget what they lost, you understand?"

Marjorie understood completely and felt a pang of loss at the thought Fletcher wasn't as clean cut as he'd appeared. No wonder he could afford to rent such a nice house, have the latest laptop for his studies, and spend up to fifteen dollars a day in a café. When she turned to Duncan, she saw the disappointment reflected in his eyes.

"How often do you come by things that need storing?" she asked, biting on her bottom lip.

"Not often," Efron admitted reluctantly. "But they need housing for a long time when we do happen upon them."

"Why don't you just hire a storage unit?" Duncan said while his face flushed with anger. "Why involve my brother in this scam at all?"

"Storage units come with CCTV watching twenty-four, seven. There's no way to hide from them, at least not in this town. But a rental house?" He shrugged. "Nobody looks twice at a moving van parking in the driveway for a few hours, loading or unloading."

Marjorie exchanged a glance with Duncan. "Do you know anything about Fletcher's disappearance?" she asked. "More than you've told me already?"

"I swear." Efron spread his arms wide. "If I thought there was some connection, I'd 'fess up."

"What about your packages?" Duncan asked in a low growl. "Any of those have additional goodies hidden away in them? Something that might lead to a lot more jail time than just a few misplaced appliances."

"I don't know—"

"For goodness' sake," Marjorie said, slamming her palm on the table. The ferocity startled her as much as it did Efron. "There's been a major drug bust in town on the same day Fletcher went missing and you expect us to believe you don't know what we're talking about?"

"N-nothing like that. I swear it."

"You swear an awful lot of things for someone who's been cheating, lying, and stealing for years." Duncan fixed the man with a steely stare, pointing his finger at Efron's eyes. "If I find out you've been holding something back, and it harms my brother…"

Although he let the threat trail off, it seemed Efron didn't need any further illumination. He swallowed hard, pressing his pale lips together in a thin line.

"Come on," Duncan said, tapping Marjorie on the shoulder. "I don't want to stay in this place one second longer than I have to."

It was a sentiment Marjorie wholeheartedly agreed with. As they let themselves out the front door, she wondered what her sleepy little town had come to. Missing persons, drug busts, and now this bumbling fool turned out to be a criminal fence.

"We should tell the police," she said once they were back in Fletcher's house. "No matter what we promised Efron. I can't believe Fletcher's involvement isn't connected to his disappearance."

But Duncan didn't agree. "How about we leave it a bit longer?" He sat down in his brother's bedroom, eyeing the stack of boxes with hatred. "Efron seemed to be telling the truth about that much at least."

"Considering he must lie regularly, I'd say he's good at it."

Duncan buried his face in his hands. "But if this genuinely has nothing to do with it, then I've stitched my twin up for nothing."

Marjorie sat on the bed beside him, wanting to say something reassuring but not having the words. "I suppose if you'd stayed in a motel as you'd planned, we never would've found this equipment."

Duncan shot her a grateful glance. "And you wouldn't have seen the neighbour acting suspiciously."

The idea didn't sit well with Marjorie but neither did hurting Duncan when he'd already suffered an enormous loss. Besides, promising not to tell the police didn't exclude her from having a casual chat with an old friend about a theoretical situation, did it?

Regina would still be at work now, but if Marjorie called by her place in a few hours, she'd be free. In the meantime...

"The kitchen is empty," she said, pulling Duncan into a safer topic. "Why don't we go shopping and make sure you've got enough stuff to get by for the next few days? Even if you're not feeling hungry now, you'll be glad of it later."

They set off on foot, Duncan so distracted Marjorie had to stop him from stepping out in front of a car.

"Sorry," he said, shaking his head. "I guess after my sleepless night, coffee should be top of the shopping list."

"Or bottom." Marjorie frowned. "If you drink it at this late hour, you'll be wired when it comes time to go to bed. How about a nice Ovaltine instead?"

He sniggered. "Sure, grandma. Whatever you say."

She elbowed him in the ribs, glad to see his mood improving, even at her expense.

"Hey, you!"

Marjorie turned, surprised to see Fletcher's professor bearing down upon them. What was his name?

"Tyrone. Nice to meet you again," she said, stepping forward before the man quite reached them. She held out her hand, but he ignored it, staring with disgust at Duncan.

"I don't know what you think you're up to, Fletch," Tyrone shouted. "But you'd better stop it right this instant or you'll be in more trouble than you know what to do with."

Duncan backed up a step, holding his hands out to ward off the man. "Look, I don't know what you want—"

"Oh, don't you?" Tyrone shoved past Marjorie and stuck his face into Duncan's. "We have an agreement, remember? If you don't start living up to your part of the bargain, things won't end well."

"This is Fletcher's brother, Duncan," Marjorie said in a loud voice. "He came to town after I reported him missing to the police. Do you have some information on his whereabouts?"

Tyrone spun on his heel, nostrils flaring. "What are you babbling about? I don't know who you're trying to fool, but I know Fletcher better than you think." He turned back, poking a finger hard into Duncan's chest. "Don't I?"

Duncan pulled out his wallet, flipping it to the clear envelope with his driver license photo. "I'm Fletcher's twin brother and nobody's trying to trick you. Do you mind if we ask you a few questions?"

In a second, the high emotion drained from Tyrone's face. "You're his twin? He never told me he had a brother."

"And yet, here I am." Duncan tucked his wallet back into his jeans pocket. "Now, who are you?"

"This is Fletcher's professor," Marjorie said, her nerves jumping like popcorn in hot oil. "Tyrone Jasper, is that right?"

The man turned to her with eyes that were unfocused and confused.

"I've met you before," Marjorie prompted him. "Although Fletcher whisked you away before we could talk more than bare introductions."

Tyrone nodded. "You're the café owner, right? I remember." He turned back to Duncan, clearing his throat. "Sorry about coming at you like that. I've had a few very stressful days, and it's affecting me more than I thought." He stepped away. "I'll let you get back to it."

"Wait," Duncan called out, but the man just waved over his shoulder and got into a nearby car. Marjorie walked a few steps towards him, but he accelerated away from the curb.

"You know him?" Duncan asked as she rejoined him. "Do you know where he lives?"

"No, but with a name that distinctive, he should be easy enough to find in the phone book or online."

They continued to the supermarket where Marjorie steered him towards every foodstuff he mentioned. After they'd finished and returned to Fletcher's house, Duncan asked her if she wanted a lift home.

Checking her watch, Marjorie saw it was now after five. Regina should be finished with work, swapping her uniform for civvies and due to head out the back door of the station in just a few minutes. "I'm good. I think I'll call in on a friend and she'll sort me out with a ride home."

Marjorie parted from him with a goodbye wave, hoping Duncan wouldn't feel too betrayed by what she was about to do.

# CHAPTER EIGHT

"I can put a few feelers out," Regina said, sitting back and breaking a chocolate chip biscuit into bite-sized pieces. "With the equipment make and model, we should be able to find something in the records."

"What if the original owners didn't report the theft?"

"Don't worry about that. They need the police case number to file an insurance claim for the loss. Unless they're made of money, it'll be on our books somewhere."

She looked unhappy as she said the words

and Marjorie followed the thought home. "But it doesn't get you any closer to tracking down the original thieves."

"Exactly. From your description, even the neighbour won't be at the top of the chain. And I can't see why he'd do a runner when the equipment's sitting right there, in his flat."

Marjorie felt the sting of dejection and when Monkey Business nosed his way into her lap, she welcomed the attention. When she'd caught up with Regina outside the police station, her friend had accepted her offer to drive her to the café. In return, she'd leave with an ample supply of baking. For herself, or to share with workmates if she needed to curry favour.

"From what I can see, you've no real reason to worry." Regina tapped her fingers on the table and frowned out the window at the darkening sky. "Although it seems weird for Fletcher to stay out of contact for a while, there's no sign of foul play. Even if criminal activity forced him into doing a runner, I doubt anything bad happened."

"Do people often disappear with no explanation?"

"All the time. Even here, I've probably taken one or two missing person reports every week since starting back, and we don't have a large population. People, especially men, will go walkabout for a while, clearing their head or clouding it with alcohol."

"But how can someone just pick up and leave like that?" Marjorie pulled her best schoolmistress impression, making Regina laugh.

"They're not thinking of anyone else is why. Not everyone wears responsibility well."

"I hope that's all it is, then." Marjorie sighed and pressed her finger against the crumbs on her plate, transferring them to her tongue. "I'd much rather be worried because Fletcher's a thoughtless young man than because anything bad happened to him."

"Amen to that."

Chaplin gave up his patrol of the windowsill long enough to jump into Regina's lap. Once there, he gave a gigantic yawn and padded at her legs before falling asleep.

"Does that mean I have to stay forever?" she asked, winking at Marjorie. "Is this your cunning plan to adopt out all your temporary residents?"

Marjorie held up her hands. "I never force anybody to do anything they don't want to." She gave the kitten a closer examination. "The only thing I'm surprised about is him falling asleep when it's near dinner time."

The ragdoll cracked open one eyelid, staring up with a hopeful expression.

"You little faker," Regina said, laughing as she picked him up around the middle and placed the kitten back on the floor. "I'd better head off, though I won't need dinner after those cupcakes." She patted her stomach with a satisfied grin.

After she'd gone, Marjorie sat and stared down the valley, watching the shadows grow until the streetlights flicked on, all at once, spreading artificial yellow light across the roads. When the section next door was cleared, she'd have the same view from the counter. A treat to look forward to before the noise and bustle of the real build began.

"But that's all in the future," she said to Monkey Business as he sauntered into the café with an expression of deep concern on his face. "Let's get you all fed."

The kittens agreed with that idea.

TUESDAY MORNING'S alarm jerked Marjorie out of a dream where she'd abandoned everyone she'd ever known and loved to live a life on the road, carefree of all obligations.

It was a nightmare. The hollow feeling in her stomach continued, despite helping herself to an extra egg with her morning toast.

As she waited for the first round of muffins to rise in the oven, she stole a glance at Esme's massage studio, wishing her friend was over there right now. She'd love to have a chat and hash through the disturbing situation.

Jerry had given her carte blanche to contact them during their holiday, but Marjorie would never cross that line unless things grew desperate. A break-in or a house fire, sure. She'd get right on the phone. Apart from that, she'd leave them in peace.

Still, it didn't stop her from imagining a conversation. Even abandoned, Esme's studio looked warm and inviting.

The oven dinged, and by the time Marjorie had a batch of scones inside, browning nicely, the pall had lifted. A quick play with the kittens—just to keep them in top form—buoyed her spirits even further.

It would be a lovely day. She'd put all the nonsense associated with Fletcher's disappearance behind her and spend her care on the customers who turned up at the café, not the one who was missing.

With soft music playing in the background, and a treat cupcake adding the spice of naughtiness to her morning, Marjorie brewed a coffee and leaned against the outside wall after placing out her open sign, breathing in the dewy morning air.

"Have I snagged the good table again?" Cecelia asked, getting out of her car.

Marjorie nodded and opened the door for her first client, shooing the kittens away from the inside door before any of them could escape.

A busload of tourists kept her occupied later in the morning. The unexpected arrivals took so many photos, the café resembled a disco with strobe lighting.

Although the business was nice, she couldn't take a full breath until the café emptied out again. The slow pace of her usual workday was something she'd grown used to and, apart from the extra money in her till, Marjorie preferred to keep it that way.

"What's this kitten's name?" an elderly woman called out near closing time. She had Chaplin on her lap, though the ragdoll's eyes were firmly fixed on a blackbird hopping outside the window.

"He's Chaplin," Marjorie replied, "because

of the…" She touched her philtrum, where the kitten had a streak of black.

"If I were ten years younger, I'd fill out that application in a shot," the woman said, her voice cracking with regret. "But even with Nurse Maude lending a hand, I doubt I'll see the year out in my own place."

"Do you have a home picked out?" Marjorie asked. "There's some that have lovely facilities nowadays."

"Yeah. I've got my eye on one or two in my price range." She leaned over to the side, offering her hand to shake. "My name's Gwen."

"Please to meet you, Gwen. I'm Marjorie."

The woman burst into laughter, shaking her head. "I might be getting doddery but even I can read your signs."

"Fair enough."

"What would happen to a kitten if its owner went into an assisted living facility?"

"It depends on the contract, but I think most of them exclude pets. Especially if you're living in the hospital section. Even if the staff are on board with picking up after animals, there'll be patients who're allergic or too delicate for a rambunctious cat."

"I'd guess that too," Gwen said, giving Chaplin a final stroke before putting him down on the floor. "It's a pity there's not a facility to give pet visits."

And just like that, Marjorie's mind dinged with a fresh idea. "I wonder if a retirement home would be happy with someone popping in once or twice a week and taking the kittens away after a few hours of interaction."

Gwen's eyes twinkled. "Oh, I wonder too. Is there someone in our community who'd be willing to give a program like that a try?"

As Marjorie counted out the woman's change, her mind was already clicking through the safety procedures she'd need to ensure were in place. An emergency plan for AWOL kittens at the end of visits. A form to be completed by residents to make sure no one ended up with an asthma attack from being in the wrong place at the wrong time.

So many studies had shown that

interaction with animals helped the elderly to live stronger, better lives. It wouldn't take much persuading for a facility director to have their arm twisted into giving such a scheme a trial run.

"Let me know if you set it up," Gwen said, reading her mind. "If there's a home who doesn't mind having kittens to visit, they'll get my vote."

Marjorie had jotted down a few ideas when the bell above the door tinkled. Right on the dot of closing. She looked up with concern, wondering if it was possible to just tell the customer she'd missed out, but the young redheaded woman standing in front of her seemed too distressed to try out the option.

"What'd you want to try?" she asked instead, apparently flummoxing the new arrival.

"My name's Vicky Wendall," the young woman said instead of naming food or selecting a coffee. "When I went to the police station today, I overheard your name being mentioned and thought you might help."

"Take a seat, love," Marjorie said, noticing the woman was swaying back and forth. While she ran around the counter, Vicky collapsed into a chair. "What is it you think I can help you with?"

"Fletcher Byrne. I heard a policewoman say you'd reported him missing."

"I did, although I'm surprised someone told you that."

"Nobody told me," Vicky said with a vague hand flap. "I just eavesdropped. My ears picked up on it because I'd gone to the police station to do exactly the same thing." She straightened in her chair, her green eyes staring straight into Marjorie's. "You see, I'm Fletcher's girlfriend and I haven't seen or heard from him in nearly a week."

# CHAPTER NINE

Marjorie's eyes dropped to the floor while her mind spun in circles. Did Adelaide know about this woman? Monkey Business padded over and demanded attention, giving her the perfect excuse to sit down and pull him into her lap. He always sensed when she needed company.

"You know Fletcher, don't you?" Vicky asked, her brow crinkling in concern. "Or did I get that wrong?"

"No, you're right. I know Fletcher and I'm the one who reported him missing. Sorry for seeming vacant. I was just about to close when you walked in."

"Oh. I'll go." The young woman sprang to her feet like a jack-in-the-box with a brand-new spring. All traces of her earlier unsteadiness were gone. "I didn't think."

"Sit down, Vicky. You're fine. I didn't mean to imply otherwise. What did you want to know about Fletcher?"

"Well, I guess what you've told the police. Why did you think you should report him?"

The question struck a false note with Marjorie, but she didn't see the harm in answering. It briefly flashed across her mind that Vicky might be a journalist, digging around for a story. In which case, she'd soon find herself out of luck.

"I guess for the same reason you went down there today. He hadn't been in for a few days and when I visited his house, I got worried."

"Because of the stuff stored in his bedroom?"

Marjorie's eyes jerked up to meet Vicky's, shocked. "You know about the computers?"

"Sure. I'm his girlfriend, aren't I? I know about everything he gets himself into."

"Well, I meant the..." Marjorie trailed off as she remembered she'd decided to file a report after meeting Adelaide. Unable to think of a lie at short notice, she gestured vaguely and fixed her attention back on the Persian in her lap.

"Do you know when he went missing?"

"The last anybody saw of him was Wednesday. How about you?"

"Yeah." Vicky pulled her phone out and tapped the base on the table. "Same. I've sent him a few texts on our special number but got nothing in return."

"What special number?"

"Hm?" Vicky's eyes were glazed with memory as she glanced at Marjorie. "Oh, just... Fletcher's got a second SIM card on his phone and I use that rather than his regular one. That way, he always knows it's me."

Oh, dear. Marjorie shook her head as she

thought of poor Adelaide, communicating with her boyfriend on a public Facebook page while this young lady sent him messages by stealth.

"You should take the sign in," Vicky said out of nowhere. When Marjorie raised her eyebrows, not following, the woman nodded to the car park. "I'm not the only one to turn up late."

With horror, Marjorie saw Duncan pulling up outside, Adelaide sitting in the passenger seat. "I'll just tell them," she said, setting Monkey on the floor before she hurried out the door. "What are you two doing here?"

"We wanted someplace to stay where we could talk openly about Fletcher," Adelaide said, sliding out of the car.

Her eyes were red-rimmed in a face free of makeup. Marjorie guessed the poor girl had learned mascara didn't team well with emotional turmoil. "I've just got a last customer of the day," she said, fumbling for the magic words to stop the oncoming encounter. "How about I meet you in town later?"

"You don't mind us stopping by, do you?" Duncan asked. Since the day before, his cheeks had turned sunken, dark circles under his eyes spreading like sad warpaint. "We can leave."

The dejection in his voice was too much for Marjorie to bear. Just as she hadn't kept Fletcher's secret stash of computer equipment to herself, neither should his second girlfriend be something she took on the burden of hiding.

"Don't be silly," she said in a chiding tone, giving him a push towards the entrance. "Go on inside. Adelaide, could I have a quick word?"

The woman raised her eyebrows, her mouth trembling. "Has something bad happened?"

Marjorie took her arm and walked a few steps towards Esme's rooms. "There's a young woman in the café called Vicky Wendall. Have you heard of her?"

Adelaide shook her head, her mouth pulling down at the corners. "No. What's this about?"

"She claims to be Fletcher's girlfriend."

Marjorie expected more tears but the young woman's face hardened like steel. "Oh, does she?" Adelaide pulled her arm free and strode towards the entrance. "We'll see about that."

Houdini crept outside, slinking through the entrance as Adelaide walked in. Marjorie scooped him up before he could run farther, holding him tightly while he protested his capture.

"I'll just stash this kitten away," she said, heading for the stairs. "Think about what you want to drink and I'll put on a round of tea and coffee when I come back down."

Adelaide and Vicky were in the middle of a staring war, seated opposite each other at the table. She didn't think they'd heard a single thing and gave a sigh thinking of how awkward the next few minutes—or hours —would be.

"So much for a quiet night alone at home," she muttered to Houdini as she walked over to the crate. If the Chartreux couldn't learn to stay inside, she'd have to keep him contained for his own safety. However, when she fumbled the door open, Marjorie changed her mind.

The kitten's face was so downcast, she couldn't add to his burden by trapping him in a small cage. Of every kitten she'd had the pleasure of fostering, he was the one who most yearned to be free.

"Okay," she said, closing the door again and setting the grey cat inside the playpen. "But no more escaping tonight, okay? Mummy needs a break."

She stroked the kitten's head, and his golden eyes glowed at her with brief contentment. When she took her hand away, he mewed in protest, starting up a chain reaction with the other residents.

"I have guests downstairs," Marjorie explained to no avail. "I can't just leave them alone."

But she could. It wasn't as though she'd invited them to be there.

Marjorie sat at the top of the stairs, Monkey Business finding her newly located lap with his powerful kitten radar. Although her mother would turn in her grave at the thought, she didn't feel any twinges of guilt eavesdropping on the conversation.

When everyone downstairs had calmed down, walking back into their midst would be an option. Until then, she'd be a little pitcher with big ears.

"Anybody who really knew Fletcher would know he spent a lot of his nights at the Poolside Tavern," Adelaide said with an edge to her voice. "I bet even Duncan knows that and he lives a ninety-minute drive away."

Duncan mumbled something noncommittal and Marjorie smiled. Good boy. Stay out of the middle of this argument and it would all blow over rather than continue to blow up.

"At least I know how to message him when he doesn't want desperate pleas written all over his Facebook page. From the time I've spent with Fletcher, he appreciates restraint."

"And I know he wouldn't be seen dead with someone who dresses in Salvation Army rags." Adelaide gave a giant sniff as punctuation. "Fletcher had such an acute sense of style, I'm not surprised you were skulking around on the down-low. Who'd want to be seen in public with someone who thinks an ensemble is a band?"

"The man *I* know doesn't wallow in artificial societal constructs like being a slave to fashion or the race to own the latest gadget. He prefers depth and intelligent debate. No wonder he needed to foster a relationship with a woman of substance instead of a barbie doll, dressing up like her world got stuck in playtime."

"I've gotta say, none of these sounds like my brother at all." Duncan drummed his fingers on the table. "And I'm not sure you two bickering offers any clues where he might hide. Don't either of you have any solid information?"

Marjorie pressed the back of her hand against her mouth to stop laughing. The man was reacting out of the depths of his grief and worry so no one could hold it against him. Still, the harsh response delighted her.

"Time to make a reappearance," she told Monkey, setting him free to peruse the sofa. He liked to stick his nose far down into the cracks between the cushions. Once, she'd lost him for a few hours to the back of the couch, only seeing his pleading eyes when she came over to sit down.

"Have you thought what you'd like to drink?" Marjorie called out in a loud voice, descending the staircase. "I'll bring over a plate with the leftovers from today."

"No, thanks," Adelaide said, patting her flat stomach as though it repulsed her. "I'm still stuffed from lunch."

Vicky tipped her nose in the air, not bothering to respond at all.

"I'd love a latte if it's not too much bother," Duncan said. "But you must let me pay this time."

"You can pay once your brother's found," Marjorie said, slipping in behind the counter. "And I don't charge after hours. Not for my guests."

"Even when they barge in on you," he said with a grin, showing a degree of self-awareness. "Seriously, thank you."

"It's just bean water and milk. No thanks required." She brought a plate of scones and cupcakes, denying the local piggery of the pleasure, and their drinks. With a hot mug of chai warming her hands, Marjorie turned them back to the main subject. "What new information have you learned today?"

Duncan ran a hand through his hair and huffed out a breath. "Nothing on my part. How about you?"

*I found out your brother has another girlfriend.* "I completely forgot to research the professor we bumped into yesterday," Marjorie said, clapping a hand down on the table. "Did you?"

"No." He whipped his phone out and typed while Marjorie envied his dexterity. Even with Swype enabled, her words often came out as pure gibberish. "There's nothing here."

"What's the name?" Adelaide asked, frowning. "I've never heard Fletcher mention his professors."

Vicky raised an eyebrow and leaned forward, only to find Marjorie raising a warning finger near her face. "Let's not get back into one-upmanship. The name's Tyrone Jasper. I would've thought he'd be the only one with that name in the country."

At the name, Vicky's face drained of colour and she bit at her thumbnail. The young woman pulled her phone out and began tapping away, the screen hidden under the table.

"I've heard him mention the man before," the redhead muttered but Marjorie could only make out the words because she sat right next to her. To the other side of the table, they'd be lost beneath her breath.

"Massey University, wasn't it?" Marjorie asked, typing the name in before getting any confirmation. A link to the list of staff members was on the side and it only took two goes before her clumsy thumbs passed the correct message to her phone screen. "Nope. Not listed."

"Well, he wouldn't necessarily be from Massey," Adelaide said in a hesitant voice. Her eyes skittered towards Vicky's face then jerked away. "Especially not if you met him in town. We're a long way from Palmerston North."

"But I just searched generally," Duncan protested. "It didn't bring up any straight matches. Not for New Zealand."

Marjorie jerked as her phone rang while she was holding it. "Excuse me." She moved away from the table before answering. The screen only showed private, the number withheld.

"It's me here," Regina said in a strained voice. "We're at Fletcher's house, looking for Duncan, but he's out. I wondered if he was with you."

"Yeah, he's here." Marjorie moved farther back behind the counter, hooking her shoulder over to shield her whisper. "Along with two of Fletcher's girlfriends. Do you want me to pass the phone over?"

"No. Just keep him there if you can and ask him where he's going if not. I'm heading straight for your place with Sergeant Matthewson."

"Are we in danger?"

"I'd tell you if you were." Regina hung up the call before Marjorie could question her further. She glanced over at the table where Duncan was staring at his phone as though it had insulted him. Her stomach performed a cartwheel, and she pressed her hand against it.

Bad news. The tension in Regina's voice heralded bad news.

Although Marjorie tried to convince herself not to worry unnecessarily, Regina and her Sergeant arrived in a few minutes. Their faces were grim as they asked Duncan to step outside the café.

"What's happening?" Adelaide asked, her voice shrill with fear. She moved closer to

Marjorie, grabbing hold of her wrist. "Do you think they've found Fletcher?"

Duncan staggered back a step, as though hit by an invisible blow. He turned and stared through the window; his features pinched together.

A minute later, Regina led the trio inside, nodding to Marjorie. "It's not good news, I'm afraid. We've found Fletcher's car. It's submerged in the river."

# CHAPTER TEN

The sun was close to setting as Marjorie stood near Duncan on the bridge. It was on private property, though the signposts at the entrance allowed strangers to use the land as a crossing point, provided any visitors remembered to close the gate.

On one side, the bridge had a strong concrete balustrade protecting any passing vehicles from driving over the side. On the other, wires strung along robust wooden posts had done the same, until they'd snapped under the weight of a vehicle.

If only the crossing had been on the main

road, someone would have spotted the breakage sooner, which would have led them to the vehicle lying beneath the shade of the bridge. But the farmer was deep in the tail end of lambing season and it took a few days for a tourist using a shortcut to discover the accident.

Adelaide and Vicky stood shoulder to shoulder a few metres away—an odd positioning for the women who'd sniping at each other just an hour before. Marjorie stuck fast to Fletcher's brother, trying to stop horrible thoughts running through her mind.

"You can head on home, if you want to," Duncan offered for the dozenth time since they'd arrived. "I'm fine to stay around here by myself."

Marjorie gave his shoulder a quick squeeze and murmured something noncommittal under her breath. The man didn't look at all fine and the thought of abandoning him to stand guard alone while the police fished his brother's vehicle out of the river made her shudder.

"He's a good swimmer." Duncan hugged himself, his cotton shirt no match for the stiff breeze blowing straight off the water. "Mum used to call him her fish boy when we were holidaying up at Queen Charlotte Sound. Fletcher just couldn't get enough of the water."

She didn't bother to say anything. A reality check would come soon enough, courtesy of the police divers working to free the wreckage. He didn't need an anticipatory one from her.

Some part of him must already realise a car crash off the side of the bridge might incapacitate even the hardiest of swimmers. Even a brief stint of unconsciousness could have taken away Fletcher's only hope of escape. "The current doesn't look all that strong."

Considering the divers couldn't stand in the shallows of the river, despite it only being waist-deep, Marjorie thought otherwise. The car must be wedged in tight to still be in position, this many days after the crash.

A movie short played in her mind—a car plummeting off the side of a bridge into the depths of a river. She'd seen versions of the same footage so many times, the vision came easily. What came less easy was shutting it out of her head despite knowing it would just set her nerves further on edge.

"I'm fine if you want to go."

"And I'm fine staying right here until you decide you want to leave," Marjorie said in a firm voice. "Don't worry about me. I'm old and ugly enough to take care of myself."

Regina waved to her from a position fifty metres up the riverbed. Sergeant Matthewson was talking to the dive team captain, his shoulders held in a tense line.

Marjorie waved back, then fished her mobile out of her pocket. She hadn't lied when telling Duncan she'd stay beside him until the bitter end, but it didn't mean she had to do it alone. Braden's number was on speed dial and she stepped a few feet away to make the conversation as private as possible.

To her relief, Braden seemed happy to give

up an evening of tinkering on computers to come and keep her company. Seeing Duncan clutch at himself again, Marjorie also asked if he could throw a spare jersey or two into the car. "We came down here so quickly, it didn't occur to any of us to dress for the conditions."

Ten minutes later, Braden pulled up on the rest area to the side of the bridge and emerged, waving an armful of coats, sweaters, and cardigans in his hands. "I raided the boxes I've had packed and ready for the donation centre for the past few years," he admitted with a sheepish grin, distributing the goodies. "What's a loss for the Sallies is a gain for your friends."

Adelaide broke free of her rival to stay near Marjorie and Braden. Vicky remained where she was, not even coming over to check out the warmer clothes on offer.

"I'm sorry, mate," Braden said, shaking Duncan's hand and clapping him on the shoulder. "This whole situation sucks."

A shout from below had them all crowding up to the rails. The crane sitting on the bank now had its hook through the front window of Fletcher's car, slowly dragging it upright.

As the bonnet lifted above the level of the water, a shout from the opposite bank brought the progress to a halt. "Let it drain," Sergeant Matthewson yelled, trying to replicate the thought with erratic gestures.

The setting sun hit the expanse of water, lighting it with a glittering array of pinks and yellows. Against the deep green of the bushes lining the banks and the tussock covered mountains rising on either side, the image was spectacular.

The view should have been the backdrop to a love story or an inspiring tale about woes being overcome by righteous action. Instead, Fletcher's rusting car drizzled water back into the river; a frightful patter of rain.

*His body is probably lying on the front seat.*

Marjorie bit down on her tongue, using the pain to shut down the thoughts. She grabbed Braden's hand and clamped it hard— so hard he winced. The taste of iron and sweetness filled her mouth. She'd drawn blood.

"It doesn't even look like his car," Duncan said in a voice that shot up the scales. "His was different."

Braden sent Marjorie a questioning glance, and she shook her head. "They checked the number plate," she whispered to him. "It's registered to Fletcher."

She didn't add it was the same vehicle Efron had witnessed driving away from the house on Wednesday. No matter how different, how jarring it appeared in this setting, there wasn't a question it belonged to the missing young man.

After a good ten minutes of no action, Sergeant Matthewson gave another hand signal, and the crane lifted the car farther from the water. This time, rather than pausing, it continued the motion, swinging it to the side until the operator deposited it on the riverbank.

Marjorie ducked her head to avoid seeing something that would stay etched in her memory long after this moment was gone. Her glance only took in the myriad cracks across the windscreen, obscuring the view inside the car.

"Do you think we should go down there?" Duncan asked. "I feel like I should be nearby if Fletcher's inside."

"Stay here, mate," Braden said, reaching out an arm and pulling the younger man close. "If the police want your input, they'll come here and ask."

Behind them, Vicky kicked at a pebble, sending it skidding across the bridge until it hit against the curb. A farm vehicle, far off in the distance, reminded the group they were standing on a road and they all moved to the side as though ordered.

"Can I talk to you for a minute?" Adelaide asked, grabbing hold of Marjorie's free hand. "I have something important to tell you."

With a nod, Marjorie escorted her a few metres along the bridge, almost to the centre piles.

"There's no way that woman is Fletcher's girlfriend."

Marjorie held back a sigh and glanced over her shoulder. Vicky leant over the railing of the bridge, getting a closer view at the recovered vehicle.

"I can't comment on that. All I know is what she told me."

"But don't you think it's weird? The timing and all. She acts like she knows everything there is to know about Fletcher but none of it's personal." Adelaide rubbed at the side of her face and shivered. "Like she talked lots about the equipment he was holding in the bedroom but didn't know the first thing about his brand of aftershave or what he was studying."

"I don't know what to tell you. If she's not his girlfriend, why on earth would she pretend to be? It's not as though it puts her in line for a cash windfall or something."

Adelaide tugged on her earlobe, turning to stare up the road. "I just thought I should mention it in case the police need to check her out." She gulped and turned back to stare at the riverbed, her eyes jumping away from the drowned car. "Or perhaps they know all about her already. She could be working undercover."

Marjorie would have scoffed at the absurd suggestion—Fletcher's small circle of disjointed acquaintances were hardly important enough to plant an officer in their midst—but she recalled her earlier impression, that the woman seemed to act more like a dispassionate journalist than a close friend and confidante.

It wasn't too great a leap from there to an undercover officer or even an informant. It fit in with Vicky's slightly off-kilter reactions along with the timing of her appearance. The longer Marjorie considered the idea, the more it made sense.

"We can talk to the police tomorrow and share your concerns," she said, touching the young woman's elbow. "But how about you stop worrying about it right now? We should be focused on Fletcher."

A tear rolled down Adelaide's cheek. "I'm scared the police will come over soon and tell me he's dead," she whispered. "It's making me feel sick. Even talking to that weirdo is better than just standing around, waiting for my world to shatter. I can't stand this."

"Me, either." Marjorie pulled the woman into a hug.

She broke away from the embrace at the sound of pebbles being dislodged and turned to see Regina climbing the steep bank to the side of the bridge. A cold hand gripped Marjorie's stomach, tightening ruthlessly. The pair hurried back to join Braden and Duncan as the officer walked towards them.

"We didn't find anybody in the car," she called out before reaching them and Duncan sagged with relief. "But it's definitely his vehicle and there are signs he was driving it at the time it went over the bank."

"Could he have made it to shore?" Marjorie asked when Duncan appeared lost for words. "Fletcher was a very good swimmer."

Regina bit her lip and glanced down at the riverbank. "Until we find him, we won't know for sure, but if he escaped the vehicle and make it out of the river, where is he?"

"We should put together a search party," Duncan said, pulling his shoulders back and standing tall. "If my brother's seriously hurt, he might be waiting for rescue."

"The sergeant is discussing matters with the dive team, but we'll raise the possibility," Regina said. From the set of her jaw, Marjorie guessed her friend didn't believe Fletcher was alive and waiting somewhere for help. "There's another thing we've discovered in the car." The policewoman glanced around at the group. "It's a delicate matter."

Duncan let Regina take his arm and escort him to the other side of the bridge. Marjorie turned to Braden with a wan expression. "I was prepared for bad news, but this doesn't feel like news at all."

"They say that not knowing what happened to someone is worse than finding them dead," Braden said with a nod.

"Who?" Adelaide shouted. "Who says that?"

"I didn't mean—"

"It's far better to still have hope he's alive and well somewhere. How dare you suggest it's not! How dare you say we'd be better off if Fletcher was dead?"

Marjorie reached out a comforting hand, but Adelaide shrugged her off and stalked down the road. The muscles of her jaw were rigid as she stared down to where the dive team captain talked with Sergeant Matthewson.

Duncan came back to stand next to Marjorie, his face turned to stone. "I'll head home now," he said in a small voice. "There's nothing for me to do here."

"You know my number if you want to chat," she said, waggling her phone. "I know it's been a long and terrible day but try to get a good sleep, if you can."

"I'll try." He issued a harsh laugh that sounded closer to a bark. "Do you know what Regina wanted to whisper to me in secret?"

She shook her head.

"They didn't find Fletcher's body in the car, but they found traces of drugs. She thinks he was transporting a large quantity of illegal substances when he drove straight off the bridge."

"Oh, no!" Marjorie grasped his hand but, when he gave no responding pressure, she dropped it.

"Turns out the equipment stashed in his room was the least of my brother's criminal activities. They suspect he was the leader of the drug ring they just busted." Duncan shook his head, his lips twisting into a scowl. "Fletcher Byrne. Drug Lord."

## CHAPTER ELEVEN

The next afternoon, Duncan walked into the café near on closing time, bringing a general sense of gloom along with him.

"The police think his body washed downstream, towards the ocean," he told Marjorie in between finishing up with the last few customers. "Although they'll keep search teams out in the area for the next few days, they've already told me to prepare for the eventuality they never recover Fletcher's body."

Although she made the appropriate noises,

nothing she said could wipe the expression of despair from the young man's face. Marjorie made do with feeding him and giving him a shot of caffeine to keep him going. Judging from the exhausted set of his shoulders, he'd got little sleep.

Once the last of the day's customers were out the door, she grabbed a glass of water for herself and sat down opposite Duncan. Chaplin sat on the windowsill nearby, keeping a sleepy eye on the birds pecking through the gravel of the car park outside while Houdini hovered, batting a small toy back and forth.

"What are the next steps?" she asked. A list of actions would make her feel useful instead of just sitting, observing his grief.

"The police told me I should inform people." Duncan's voice was twisted with misery, barely audible. "I h-have to call up everybody he ever knew and tell them he's dead."

"What about a memorial service or a funeral?"

Duncan dropped his face into his hands,

his shoulders shuddering. "I haven't thought that far ahead. Shouldn't we wait?"

"Have you called your parents?" Marjorie bit her lip as Duncan stiffened and she realised she'd never worked out if they were still alive or not.

"They're overseas," he said, shaking his head. "I-I c-can't..."

While he trailed into sobs, Marjorie placed a hand on his shoulder, pulling her phone out with the other hand. Navigating these demands was too much of a task for this young man, already devastated through the loss of his twin.

She dialled Regina's personal number, unable to think what shift she would be working by now. The brain fog of grief was affecting her, too. It was hard to believe she'd never look up from the counter to see Fletcher playing with a kitten or staring down the hill to the township, surveying everything happening with one glance.

Luckily, her friend answered, work over for the day.

"Can you come up to the café to help me?" Marjorie asked. "Duncan needs a hand informing relatives and organising things."

Although it was well outside her usual scope of operations, Regina agreed without a second thought and turned up in a few minutes, clutching a list.

"The first thing we need to do is work out who to tell first," she said, her business-like manner straightening Duncan's spine until he appeared closer to his usual self. "Your parents will be first but I've gathered a list of relatives we know about. As I read through them, tell me where they fit in the picture, then you can add any friends and family we've missed."

Marjorie slipped away, feeding the kittens and giving them extra hugs to make up for the sadness permeating the air of the café. Although their youth would soon have them putting the incident behind them, the cats were attuned to emotions and their manner was subdued.

"Once we get through this rough streak," she promised Monkey Business. "We'll do something fun to cheer everybody up and remind them why life is so precious. How about a kitten party? You can explode balloons and I'll dress up a scratching post as something worthy of your fighting claws."

With the kittens fed and replete, she headed downstairs.

"I think we're making headway," Regina said as Marjorie took the seat beside her. "I've got a couple of scripts we use at the station for informing relatives if you want to make use of those."

It took a few hours to work their way through the list. During some conversations, Duncan would tap her or Regina on the shoulder and take the phone, managing a few stumbling sentences before he became overwhelmed and handed it back.

The experience wasn't one she'd ever want to repeat but Marjorie was happy to lift the burden off the young man's shoulders. As they reached the end of the list, the mood brightened a little, one terrible task gone. More to come.

"Once your parents arrive"—they were on the next flight into the country, though being in Europe meant it was a day and a half away —"you'll be able to sit down with a funeral director and talk through the service you want to have." Marjorie reached out and touched the back of Duncan's hand. "In the meantime, think about if you want to speak and the music your brother would want to play."

"Adelaide will probably have a better idea of that," Duncan said, rubbing the back of his neck. "Or Vicky Wendall."

When he said the second name, Marjorie kept her gaze on Regina, but if the woman knew Vicky was an undercover officer, she hid it well.

As she walked Regina to her car, Marjorie asked, "What will it mean for the family, Fletcher being involved with drugs?"

"Nothing. If he was alive, then it'd be a different story, but we don't prosecute dead people for crimes." She glanced back at the café. "There doesn't appear to be any link back to his family and we've already checked and cleared his girlfriend."

"What about his next-door neighbour?"

"He's on the list for a grilling."

Marjorie told her friend about the professor they couldn't locate. Hopefully, the police would do a better job. "As Adelaide pointed out, he's unlikely to be directly involved with Fletcher's schooling." Her mouth twisted as another thought struck. "If he was even doing the distance learning thing at all."

"Oh, that part checks out." Regina hugged her goodbye.

Duncan left a few minutes later, thanking her for everything with shell-shocked eyes. Marjorie settled down on the sofa with a plethora of kitten company and it took until the room went dark for her to remember to turn on the TV.

When she went to bed, even Monkey Business wasn't enough company to keep the bad thoughts at bay. She picked her phone up from the nightstand and called Braden.

"Would you keep me company while I fall asleep?"

He agreed, though warned her he was playing a multi-player game and would be loud. The noisy voice of someone whose company she enjoyed was just what Marjorie needed, and she soon fell asleep, listening to zombies being eradicated from a post-apocalyptic planet.

"BACK UP, MONKEY," Marjorie said the next morning, pulling a steaming hot tray of cheese muffins out of the oven. "And no touching," she warned as Chaplin jumped onto the windowsill in a paper-thin pretence of looking outside. "If you get a grease burn from this hot cheese, you'll get no sympathy from me."

When her stern admonition failed to stir him, Marjorie lifted the ragdoll off the sill and placed him back in the playpen. "Stay," she said in a deep voice. "Be a good boy and I'll give you a treat later."

Marjorie had woken to a silent phone with a text message informing her that Braden had disconnected the call when her deafening snores had intruded upon his enjoyment of the game.

She sent back a text with a loud siren call, ready to blast him awake at what he considered the ungodly hour of five in the morning, sniggering as she thought of the expression of horror that would cross his face.

"Okay. The game plan today is business as usual," she told the assembled kittens. "No grieving relatives. No suspicious girlfriends. No police officers, bless their hearts. Today is for customers wanting a snack and a cup of coffee only. Now, let's see your best 'you must adopt me, or you'll regret it' faces."

What she received were a load of sleepy stares.

"That'll have to do. Luckily, each one of you has been blessed with cuteness already. Who feels like a game of catch the red dot?"

The gang pretended to ignore her until the laser pointer came out and soon had them jumping up the walls.

"Now we just need to keep up that level of energy, and I'm sure you'll score some loving admirers."

Setting out the display cabinet of freshly baked goodies took longer than usual since Marjorie kept stopping to yawn. She might have had a good night's sleep but the raw emotion of the day before had drained all her energy. "I'm like an Energiser bunny with the wrong batteries installed," she said to Monkey Business when he nudged up against her ankles.

With no chance to drop off old muffins to either of her usual recipients the afternoon before, Marjorie took the leftovers out the back to the dumpster. After a second's thought, she changed her mind, breaking the rock-hard treats into pieces and scattering them on top of the gravel for the birds.

"You'll drive Chaplin crazy," she murmured as the sparrows and starlings flocked, despite her standing nearby. With a few minutes to spare before opening, she stayed outside, a smile on her face as she watched the birds squabbling.

It wasn't until she turned to head back inside the café that she saw Houdini's face peering through the window.

Esme's window.

The rascal had broken out of his home and into the next-door neighbour's massage studio.

"No wonder they call them cat burglars," Marjorie muttered as she headed inside to grab the keys Esme had left behind.

# CHAPTER TWELVE

*I*t took two cycles through every key on the holder before Marjorie accepted the front-door key was missing. She was horrified at herself for letting it slip out of her possession and scared at what devastation she might find inside the massage rooms. Since the key could have been taken any time in the past week, thieves could have stripped the establishment down to its bare bones.

With guilt making it hard to breathe, Marjorie walked around the back of the studio, fighting back tears. To find out she'd compromised her friend's place of business—Esme's livelihood—made her nauseous. She'd only meant to leave they keyring on the downstairs hook. for the afternoon! With everything that had gone on, they'd never made it to the comparative safety of upstairs.

At least the back-door key was still on the ring. She opened the door a few inches, waiting to hear if any sounds emerged. Given the time that had elapsed, it would be silly to think burglars would be inside right now. Sillier still not to yell out and check, then find herself trapped in a sticky situation.

"My name's Marjorie Hardaway and I'm coming inside. If anybody's in here, now's your chance to run out the front door."

After another few minutes of silence, Marjorie shouted the warning again, her face colouring as she did so. It was foolish to yell when it was obvious no one was there. The only thing she'd be doing was giving Houdini a fright and the last thing she wanted was for him to become skittish.

"I'm walking inside and I have the police on speed dial."

Still nothing. Marjorie closed the back door behind her, not wanting Houdini to have a chance at escape, though since he'd obviously found another way inside, he might still slip out of her clutches.

"Hey boy," she cooed, walking into the massage room. After clicking her tongue, Houdini shot a bored expression her way before returning his gaze to the car park. "Come on over. It's time to go home."

The kitten stretched, his body angling to appear twice its usual length, then he shook out each hind leg. If he'd been a human, Marjorie would've expected him to say, "Yeah, alright. There's no hurry."

"Do I have to come over there and pick you up?" She put her hands on her hips, feigning anger. "You've got legs, use them."

Houdini trotted over and mewed, then fell onto his back on the floor, squirming as he tried to ease an itchy spot. When he seemed satisfied, he splayed his limbs out, opening up his belly.

"I wasn't born yesterday, kitty. I won't fall for that one."

With a shake of his head, Houdini rolled over, sneezing lightly then seeming astonished.

"Okay, that's enough." Marjorie hooked her hand under his belly and lifted the Chartreux kitten up to rest against her shoulder. "You're done exploring for one day. I'm just going to give all the rooms a quick check to see what's missing, then we can go back home."

What was missing was nothing. The rows of expensive massage oils were still lined up, not a bottle out of place, and the till hadn't been pried open.

A safe hid behind a locked wardrobe door, and after manhandling the kitten while finding the right keys, Marjorie verified no money had been taken. Unless Esme stashed a large emergency supply in there, all the change was in place.

"Well, perhaps the key dropped off the ring at another time," she whispered to Houdini, closing her eyes for a second in sheer relief. "But I'd better check the entire café before she gets home." Along with the vacuum cleaner. It wouldn't be the first time Marjorie had lost a small item to its powerful suction.

An upstairs window sitting a slight bit ajar looked to be the exit point from her establishment but as she dropped Houdini back into the playpen, it occurred to Marjorie she hadn't found a point of entry for the kitten. He might be wily in the extreme, but he couldn't unlock a door or open a window hinge.

"One quick check, then I'm opening," she told the kittens who were apparently more interested in spending a few minutes dozing before the day began.

With her eyes and ears on high alert, she crunched over the gravel path back to the massage studio, this time her attention fixed on the windows and doors rather than scanning the place for movement.

When she went through the back door, she kicked at the cat door marked out in the wood but the metal hinges holding it shut—cheaper than a replacement door, Esme assured her—were still firmly in place.

"If I was a gap where would I be?" she called out in a sing-song voice, then stopped dead in her tracks as she heard a floorboard creak. "Is anybody in here?" she called out, hands already fumbling for her cell phone.

A groan answered her, pitifully weak.

"Who is it?" Marjorie demanded, reaching behind her for the back-door handle, ready to run. "Who's there?"

Another low moan came, almost drowned out by the thud of her heartbeat in her ears.

She opened the door wide, wanting an easy escape if someone was playing possum and lying in wait. Marjorie laced the keys through her fingers, forming a knuckleduster with bite.

"I'm coming in," she said, edging towards the connecting door to the massage room. With a trembling hand, she pushed it open with her fingertips, revealing an empty space that looked just how she'd left it. "Where are you?"

Another groan sounded, this one louder and verging on a word. It came from the ceiling.

Marjorie backed out to the rear door, frowning at the manhole above her. A stepladder was clumsily balanced against the wall and she set it up, staring upwards with concern.

She phoned Braden. "I'm about to go into the attic of Esme's massage rooms," she said through chattering teeth. "If I don't text you in five minutes to say I'm okay, call the police."

"Wait, what?" his sleepy voice answered. "Why can't you call the police to go up there for you?"

"I think someone's up there in serious distress."

"All the more reason."

With a click of her tongue, Marjorie realised he was talking perfect sense. "Fine.

Don't worry. I'll call the police and tell them what I'm doing."

"Good," he said in a relieved voice. "And I'll stay awake until you send me a text to say what's happening."

But as Marjorie hung up the call, the groaning came again, louder. "Don't… police…"

She stepped onto the ladder, pushing up the manhole cover and shoving it clumsily to one side. "What was that?"

"Don't call the police."

With a startled cry, Marjorie stepped up the rest of the rungs, poking her head into the attic space. "Fletcher!"

"That's me."

She pulled herself up into the loft, and pulled on the light chain, sending a single bulb's illumination into the room. "What are you doing up here?" she cried out before walking over to give him a slap on the shoulder. "I thought you were dead."

"Sorry about that. Does everyone think that?"

From his dishevelled appearance, it seemed he wasn't far off. "I'm calling an ambulance," she said, pulling out her phone. "You look terrible."

"Don't!" He held up a hand. "I need to check everything's sorted before you tell the police."

"The ambulance won't…" Marjorie let the sentence die on her lips. The ambulance wouldn't call the police, but the emergency dispatcher would patch the call through, just in case.

"Are my parents here?"

"They're on their way," she snapped, feeling rage engulf her. "And thanks for letting me be the one to tell them you were dead."

He raised himself up on his elbows, then collapsed.

"What's wrong with you?" she asked, moving closer. "Where are you hurt?"

"I'm thirsty and starving," Fletcher said. "Do you have anything to eat?"

"Yeah. I always bring a picnic lunch when I go exploring," she said in an angry whisper. "If you can't get yourself down the ladder, I won't carry you down."

She backed up and reversed down the rungs, giving a puff of relief when she hit the ground. "If you're not down here in five minutes, it doesn't matter what you want. I'll call the ambulance and let the chips fall where they may."

She sent a text to Braden, telling him she was fine, then stuck the phone in her back pocket as Fletcher made the first few tentative steps downward.

"Haven't you had anything to eat since Wednesday?" she asked, horrified. "Have you had something to drink?"

"I had some water, but it ran out yesterday," Fletcher said, reaching the ground with shambling steps. "Or the day before. What day is it?"

"And you've been up there all this time?" It was an echo of the questions already asked but Marjorie just couldn't get her head around it. When he gave a weak nod, yes, she followed up with, "Did you walk here all the way from the accident?"

He started to lean to one side, so Marjorie got under his armpit and grunted as she steadied him. With shaking steps, she walked over to the café, giving a sigh of relief as she deposited him in a chair.

She handed Fletcher a glass with just a splash of water in the bottom. "Take small sips," she warned. "If you're dehydrated your stomach won't appreciate being hit with a large gulp."

As he emptied the glass, she refilled it, pleased to see his face brighten with colour. Her phone beeped as Braden sent a responding text message and she pushed it into a call. "Can you come over here right away?"

"Who's that?" Fletcher asked, squinting.

"Never you mind," Marjorie said, feeling a renewed rush of anger every time she thought of another phone call she'd made on this rat's behalf. "Do you think you can handle some food now?"

She fed him in small bites, feeling the same as when she nursed an abandoned kitten back to health. Except this youngster was big and bright enough to know better.

Judging from what she'd found out over the past week, he might also be dangerous. Marjorie felt an instant jolt of relief when Braden's sleep-deprived face popped through the front door.

"Look what I found," she said, jerking her head towards Fletcher. "Now, can you help me figure out what to do with him?"

# CHAPTER THIRTEEN

*M*arjorie didn't trust herself to make a sensible decision given how high her emotions were running. A big part of her wanted to just call Regina and let the miserable worm be led away in handcuffs. It would serve him right.

Another part told her to stay silent and listen. If she couldn't find out what had driven Fletcher into hiding, she might make the wrong choice, a decision she couldn't take back.

"Why should we listen to a word you say?"

Braden demanded when Fletcher attempted to speak. "You've put Marjorie through hell this past week, not to mention the scars you've left on your brother."

"I need to see him." Fletcher grasped Braden's hand, tugging him closer.

"Get off me." Braden jerked away, his lip curling. "I doubt Duncan will want to see you ever again, except to tell you how much you've hurt him."

"Once I explain everything, he'll understand."

"He understands you're a dead drug dealer who stashed stolen goods in his bedroom for a bit of extra cash on the side," Marjorie said in a low voice.

She stared at the table as she spoke, not trusting herself to meet Fletcher's pleading gaze. "And since he hasn't responded to the text I sent, saying you're safe, I'd guess you're not welcome. At least, not yet."

"But I'm not any of those things!"

"Then why is your bedroom full of stolen

equipment and why was your car full of drugs?"

This time Fletcher was the one incapable of holding a gaze. "Okay, there's a bit of truth in there but it's nothing as bad as what you think."

"Call the police," Braden said, slapping his palm flat on the table. "This café should be open, and I should be lying in bed, fast asleep. Any time we spend listening to this young man's feeble excuses is time wasted."

"He's going to kill me," Fletcher shouted. "That's why I had to pretend I was dead."

"Who's he?" Braden asked in return, unimpressed.

"The real drug dealer." Fletcher ran a hand through his hair, appearing on the verge of tears. "I run lookout for him, but I stuffed up. While we were out chasing a kitten, the cops swooped in and I didn't give him any notice to hide his stash or run."

"That's what you were doing in here every day?" Marjorie asked, not bothering to hide her disappointment. "Operating as a lookout for a bunch of dangerous drug dealers?" She shook her head. "And to think I let you near my kittens."

"I'm not a bad guy," Fletcher insisted. "I just got in over my head."

"How does a good guy end up faking his own death and causing his loved ones a boatload of grief?" That was Marjorie's sticking point. She just couldn't believe anyone could be so self-centred. "Why didn't you let them in on the plan?"

"Because it had to look real. If Duncan turned up, cheerful as chips, Tyrone would take one glance and know the entire thing must be fake."

"Tyrone!"

"What? You know him?" Fletcher stared at Marjorie, who nodded.

"You introduced me to him once and then Duncan and I bumped into him on the street."

"I forgot about that." The young man hugged himself, the gesture so similar to Duncan that Marjorie almost smiled. Almost.

"Is he the drug dealer?" Braden asked.

When Fletcher said yes, he added, "Couldn't you just turn him into the police?"

Fletcher stared down at his hands. "I hoped I could get out of everything. All I've wanted for the past few weeks is to walk away and never meet any of his gang again. They roped me into the whole thing by threatening to turn me in to the police over the stolen gear. It seemed like wholesale irony to turn myself in voluntarily."

"But you're already in trouble with the police, now." Marjorie stood and stretched, starting off a brief calisthenic session amongst the kittens. "Since you have to take responsibility, why not dob him in?"

"There's more than just him."

"Efron?" she guessed but Fletcher shook his head.

"I doubt he'd cause any trouble, even though he fences the stolen goods for the same gang." He shrugged. "I know Tyrone's got people in place throughout the area, but I don't know who. I'll be in danger as soon as they find out I'm not dead."

"That's what witness protection is for." Marjorie sat down again, taking Fletcher's hands between her own. "You can ask the police to protect you."

"I thought that was just an American thing."

Braden nodded and cleared his throat. "No, they have it here, too. We just don't dedicate as many TV dramas to it. It's a good idea. They can move you away from here, give you a new identity. Tyrone will get the justice he deserves, and you get to start over."

"I'll have to give up my family, won't I?" Fletcher pulled his hands back, clenching them together so hard the tendons popped out on his wrists. "They won't let me stay in touch."

"Probably not." Marjorie leaned against Braden's shoulder, grateful for his comforting warmth.

Fletcher squared his shoulders and looked her in the eye. "In that case, do you mind if I visit Duncan first? If I'm never going to see him again, I'd at least like the chance to explain."

Marjorie and Braden exchanged a look. "Okay," she said after a pause. "But if he doesn't want to see you, we're heading straight for the police. Likewise, if he's not at home. We're not traipsing around town all day trying to track him down."

"But—"

"The police will allow him to visit," Braden said in a gentler tone, making Marjorie feel like the bad cop in the situation. "Even if you don't see him now, you'll see him before they hide you away."

"Okay." Fletcher bowed his head forward, then gave a jolt and stared down with a smile. "Hello, little rascal. I suppose you won't be able to come along with me, either."

Houdini purred and placed his forelegs high up Fletcher's calves. When the young man petted him, his eyes closed in satisfaction.

"I guess I've disappointed everyone," he

said with a catch in his voice. "And I swear, I never meant to."

"Actions speak louder than intentions," Braden said, standing up and striding towards the door. "Do you want to stay here and mind the café while we get this done?"

"Not on your life," Marjorie said, quickly altering the sign with chalk and popping it outside. "I don't trust him to do what he promises at all," she whispered to Braden as she hooked her arm through his.

When they pulled up outside Fletcher's home, he stared at the property, swallowing hard before he let himself out of the vehicle. "It doesn't look any different," he said in a small voice. "I thought everything would've changed."

"You're the one who's changed." Marjorie hesitated a moment, then led the group up the front path, sensing Fletcher's reluctance. "Everything else is exactly the way you left it."

She knocked on the front door, hoping the lack of response to her text was because

Duncan was finally getting a good night's sleep rather than wanting to ignore his brother. "Yoo-hoo," she called out when nobody answered.

"There's a key around the side," Fletcher said, scooting around and returning before Marjorie could ask him where. He inserted it into the door, then frowned as he pushed it open. "It's already unlocked."

A wave of foreboding swept up Marjorie's midriff as she followed him inside, checking her phone again for any acknowledgement of her message. The house was eerily silent.

"Duncan?" Fletcher called out. "Are you here?"

He strode down the hallway, quickly checking out all the rooms, then returned to stand near Marjorie with a shrug. "He's not there. Are you sure he didn't stay at a hotel or head on home?"

"I'm not sure of anything." Marjorie frowned as she tried to think of their last conversation. "He was very upset last night but glad that we'd started planning for your funeral."

Fletcher's face blanched at her choice of words, but she wasn't about to apologise. "Is there nothing left in the bedroom?" she asked. "His suitcase or change of clothes?"

"They're still there. It's just him that's missing."

She pushed past Fletcher, checking out the empty rooms for herself. Duncan's phone sat on the bedside cabinet and when she picked it up, she saw her text on the screen. A few random letters were typed into a reply that had never been sent as though he'd been mid-answer before the phone fell from his hand.

Or was pulled away.

"Does your brother know anybody else in town?" she asked, bustling back down the corridor, her heart beating fast. "Apart from me and the police and your girlfriends."

"Eh?"

Fletcher stared at her with a quizzical expression, but Marjorie glanced over his shoulder and froze.

On the fridge, a whiteboard held a short message.

"I have your brother. Bring me the supply or he's dead."

# CHAPTER FOURTEEN

"Where is he?" Fletcher cried out in despair, pounding his fists on the table. "Why didn't he tell me where to go?"

"We need to go to the police," Marjorie said in a firm voice. "This is out of hand."

"You should never have texted him about finding me," Fletcher shouted, pointing a finger in her face. "This is all your fault."

"I think the blame lies with the man who got himself hooked up with drug dealers," Braden said in a low voice. "And I think you should sit down and think rather than yelling accusations."

"Right." Fletcher dug his fingers into his scalp and dragged them down. "I'm sorry. I don't know where he'd go. Why would he take Duncan? Surely Tyrone knows my brother is clueless about the entire operation."

"This isn't about what your brother knows." Braden paced over to examine the whiteboard. "This is about what he's worth to you."

"What's the supply?" Marjorie asked. "Does he mean the drugs that washed down the river?"

"I guess." Fletcher sounded on the verge of hysteria. "He must do. What else would he mean?" He gulped. "What if he's already killed him? What if he kills my entire family?"

"Which is why we're calling the police. Now." Braden picked up the landline and dialled.

"No!" Fletcher knocked it out of his hand, the case shattering as it hit and skidded across the floor. "No cops. If they show up outside Tyrone's house, he'll kill my brother out of spite."

"They won't let themselves be seen." Braden put his hands on his hips. "They're trained professionals."

"Oh, yes. The Hanmer Springs Police Force is widely known to be the best in the business."

"They busted your mate's drug ring."

"He's not my mate," Fletcher seethed. "And they only found the gear because someone let a kitten get loose."

"Leave Houdini out of this," Marjorie said, indignant on the Chartreux's behalf. "If you're going to work for drug dealers, you're the one responsible for keeping your mind on the job."

"They blackmailed me into doing it. I didn't 'work' for them."

Braden bristled. "Only because you made yourself vulnerable by doing something stupid."

"I needed the money from storing those stolen goods, okay?"

"We all need money."

Marjorie clapped her hands. "How about

we focus on the problem and leave the blame until Duncan's safely home?"

Fletcher nodded while Braden's cheeks coloured in embarrassment.

"Whoever left the message expected you to find him. Isn't there anywhere you can think to try?"

The young man sat, staring miserably down at his hands. "I don't know. My brain isn't working at its maximum right now."

"What about Adelaide or Vicky? Did you ever tell your girlfriends about your work? Perhaps they can remember something you can't."

"Who's Vicky?"

Braden's eyebrows drew together. "Vicky Wendall."

"Never heard of her. Are you saying she thinks she's going out with me?" He laughed. "I wish women were that eager. What's she look like?"

Marjorie gave a quick description of the redhead and Fletcher stopped laughing. "Does she have one of those rings in her eyebrow?" He pointed to his own face.

"I think so. Does that mean you do know her?"

"Yeah, but she's no friend of mine." His face grew grim. "This Vicky sounds exactly like Monica, Tyrone's fiancée. If she's been hanging around, pretending to be my girlfriend, it'll be to squeeze information out of you to report back to him."

An informant. Working for the wrong side.

Marjorie felt violated even though she'd suspected the woman wasn't who she claimed to be.

"Do you know where she lives?" When Fletcher didn't answer at once, Marjorie snapped her fingers under his nose. "Well?"

"Yeah. She's in a shared flat out near the golf course."

"Come on." Marjorie strode out of the room, giving a huff of impatience when Braden and Fletcher didn't immediately follow. "We're not going to find him in here, you two."

Once they were back on the road, Fletcher rallied. "Take a left here, then it's the third house on the right."

"But park just after it," Marjorie added. "We don't want Vicky—I mean Monica—to see Fletcher. It might be easier if I go in alone."

"Not on my watch," Braden said with such a note of finality she didn't argue.

As they observed the house for a few minutes, Marjorie quickly composed a text and sent it to Regina. Fletcher might want to keep the police out of the matter, but she wanted all the backup they could have. She added the address they were sitting outside and left her phone switched on so it would be trackable.

With that task completed, she instantly felt better about the situation. Monica had been pleasant enough in all their other encounters, even if lying, and with Braden by her side, Marjorie couldn't imagine she'd start a fight.

"Right, if we're not back out here in five minutes, run to the police station and tell them what's happening," she told Fletcher while sliding out of the back seat. "And take the keys," she prompted Braden, not trusting the young man not to drive off with the car.

When Monica answered their knock, her eyes widened, and her face grew wary. "What's happened? Have they found Fletcher's body?"

"We have," Marjorie answered with pure honesty. "But we have a problem we'd like your help to sort out. Duncan's been kidnapped but we don't know where he's being held. Since you know Fletcher so well, we thought you might have an idea."

Monica shook her head and tried to close the door, but Braden stuck his foot out to stop her. He shouldered it open again. "Tyrone's your friend, isn't he? Well, we can't give him what he wants if we can't find him."

"The old store on Spencer Street," Monica muttered, glancing back over her shoulder as another young woman wandered into the hallway behind her. "I'll just be a minute, Lucy. I'm fine." The blonde shrugged, then continued into a room on the left.

"Which number?" Braden said, tugging his phone out of his pocket. "And where's the entrance? Front or back?"

"It'll be easier if you come with us." Marjorie spread her hands out to either side. "We won't hurt you."

Monica bit on her bottom lip, frowning at the floor for a second, then nodded. "Okay. I'll just grab a jacket."

"No, you're fine how you are," Marjorie insisted, grabbing Monica's forearm and tugging her forward. "The car's air-conditioned and it's a lovely day."

She kept a firm grip on the younger woman as they walked along the footpath to the car. When Monica saw Fletcher sitting in the passenger seat, she struggled, trying to backtrack, and Marjorie let her go. "We know you're Tyrone's girlfriend," she said. "If you don't want him to see you, then you can get out of the car and walk back once you've shown us the building."

"Why doesn't Fletcher just go straight there himself?" Monica stood back a step, arms folded across her chest. "He knows the place."

"His mind's a bit cuckoo after a week in hiding." Marjorie mimicked a spiral coming out the side of her head. "But if you prompt him, he might know."

"I'm not coming, and you can't make me." Monica took another step backwards. When Braden lunged for her, Marjorie jerked at the back of his jacket.

"She's right. If you take her by force, it's kidnapping. Just the same as her friend's done to Duncan."

They got back into the car, checking the scant details with Fletcher who suddenly slapped his forehead as he remembered. Behind them, Monica walked back into the house, phone out and thumbs furiously typing.

"I guess he knows we're coming," Fletcher said in a miserable voice.

"He wants us to come," Marjorie said, slapping Braden's shoulder. "Now drive."

Like everything else in Hanmer Springs, their destination was close by. As they pulled up around the back, Marjorie checked the street. Too early for most tourists to be out and about but there were a few shopkeepers setting up their trade for the day. "How do we get in?"

"Up the fire escape and in through the back door," Fletcher said, pointing. "I'll go first."

"Yeah, you will," Braden muttered, giving Marjorie a searching look. "Are you sure you wouldn't prefer to wait in the car?"

"Quite sure, thanks."

She checked her phone just before embarking up the rusting iron fire escape. Regina had sent her a thumbs-up—whatever that meant. *Venture forth alone and get him back? I'm on my way? We're sending out a mass of troops to defend you?*

Inside, the light was muted from a storefront painted white, offering a deal on the premium rental space. Given the dust on the floorboards and the sense of gloom hanging in the air, Marjorie guessed the 'special low prices' weren't as good as the landlord seemed to think.

They crept along the mezzanine floor, each creak of the floorboards making her heart jump and her throat tighten. She wanted to pull her phone out and shout to Regina for help. Instead, she inched forward, letting Fletcher take the lead.

When they got to the staircase that led down into the shop proper, she gasped. Duncan sat on a chair, a hessian bag over his head, and his hands tied behind his back. Tyrone lounged on a sofa nearby, its fat cushions leaking stuffing onto the floor while another man—his henchman no doubt—stood at attention behind the kidnapped man.

At their footsteps, Tyrone jerked his head upward, a smile spreading across his face.

"About time, buddy. I was thinking you didn't care for your brother at all."

"Let him go," Marjorie shouted, hand tugging at the loose skin on her throat. "He's done nothing wrong."

"I'll let him go when Fletcher tells me where he's hidden my drug supply. I mean, good effort with the faking your own death and all, but I know you better than that."

Tyrone stood up, reaching down the side of the sofa and pulling out a rifle. "You can either tell me straight off and I'll send Bazza here"—he jerked his head at the other man—"along with you, or I'll start shooting holes in your brother until you give me what I need."

He lined up the rifle, nestling the butt in his shoulder and pointing the barrel at Duncan's knee.

"Wait," Fletcher yelled. "I'll take you."

Marjorie felt another rush of anger. "You said the drugs were washed away in the car."

"I couldn't risk being left empty handed if Tyrone came calling," Fletcher whispered, avoiding her eyes. "I mean, look at this." The young man turned his attention back downstairs. "Leave the goon here and I'll show you where I stashed them."

Tyrone sneered. "But I want to be the one to plug holes in your brother. If I come with you, you'll be trying to do that to me."

"How long will it take?" Marjorie asked Fletcher. "An hour?" He nodded, and she turned back to Tyrone. "If you're not back here in an hour, your goon can shoot all of us."

"What're you doing?" Braden asked, grabbing her arm and twisting her around. "We're not going to stay here with that... that thug!"

Marjorie's mobile vibrated in her pocket and a shadow passed by the painted street window. Then another.

"We'll be fine," she whispered to Braden then arched her eyebrow at Tyrone. "What'd you say?"

"Fine." He shoved the rifle into the hands of his henchman with a snarl. "You lot, come downstairs." He waited until Marjorie and Braden were standing near Duncan, then nodded to the goon. "One hour then do as the lady said and shoot everyone."

"I don't have a car," Fletcher said in a worried voice. "And I can't travel far in my current condition."

Tyrone scrunched up his face in disgust. "I've got wheels. There's even snacks and an energy drink with your name on it if you take me to my supply. My clients are hankering for product and I have nothing to give them."

They walked into an office underneath the mezzanine and didn't come back out. Marjorie shot quick snapshot glances of the goon with the rifle, calculating her chance of dying miserably before she reached the door.

Even a champion sprinter wouldn't make it in the enclosed space.

"Police!" a voice called out from above them, echoed a second later by a megaphone standing outside. "Drop your weapons and lay face down on the floor!"

Marjorie had never been so happy to lie on

dirty floorboards in her life. As her nose pressed into the dust, she saw Regina's boots walking towards her and twisted her head to look up into her friend's face. "What took you so long?"

# CHAPTER FIFTEEN

$\mathcal{B}$y the time Marjorie was let out of the police station, she'd started to think her café wouldn't open at all that day. Questions were shot at her left, right, and centre until her mind fogged up and she started to disbelieve her own answers.

Then, just as she thought this was her life now, Regina slid a transcript across the table, asked her to check and sign, and they booted her out of the door.

Full sunlight streamed down, bathing her in its light. Marjorie couldn't see from the abrupt change, but she would gladly put up with the blindness in exchange for the comforting warmth.

"Nice they didn't keep you," Braden said, waving from a park bench opposite the station. "They kicked me to the curb over an hour ago. I guess they had you pegged as the mastermind."

"Oh, it's been awful. I started to wish I was actually a criminal just to have something to confess. How many times can I say, 'I don't know where the drugs are' before it sinks in?"

Braden chuckled and pulled her into a half-hug. "Try doing it all with four hours less sleep than usual."

"Yeah, poor baby. Dragged out of bed before noon."

Regina walked out of the station and Marjorie stiffened, afraid the woman was about to drag her inside for another few rounds. Instead, she waved and jogged over to them with a concerned smile. "I forgot to say, we still haven't tracked down Fletcher and Tyrone, so take extra precautions to keep yourselves safe."

"Like what?" Marjorie stared up in confusion. "Fletcher knows where I live and work and it's not like I can move to another location. My kittens will wonder where I am as it is."

"Just double check no one's following you. Keep an eye out for strangers or people behaving oddly near you."

Braden started laughing and soon neither of them could stop. "What does that even mean?" he spurted out. "Don't get in a stranger's van even if they offer you chocolate."

"Or puppies. Or kittens," Marjorie said as her giggles tapered off. "But thanks for the warning." She added an eyeroll for punctuation.

"Where's Duncan?" Braden asked. "The sergeant just gave me a steely glance when I asked him."

"He's at the clinic getting a check-up or at home, resting. Speaking of which"—Regina aimed her finger at Marjorie's face, then Braden's—"you two should also do that."

Marjorie disentangled herself from Braden's arm with a pang of regret. "I'm heading home right now."

"And I'm coming with you. Since the other options don't sound safe, I can at least keep you company until the bad guys are arrested."

"How did Fletcher go from a victim to a bad guy in less than a week?"

"Through foolish choices," Regina said grimly. "And sticking together is a good idea. I'll pop by when I've finished my shift here to check on you."

When they pulled up outside the café, a row of worried kittens was lined up on the windowsill, staring out. "Poor babies," Marjorie said as she hurried through the doors. "I'm sorry to leave you alone for so long. I promise I only meant to take a few minutes."

The gulf between now and the morning was so wide it was hard to believe it was still the same day.

While she turned on the coffee machines and stared in dismay at her cabinets full of the morning's baking, Marjorie took a few deep breaths, centering herself.

"Oh, thank goodness," Cecelia called out, fragmenting her calm. "I've been up here a dozen times only to find the sign with a scrawled message that you'd open later. I began to think later meant sometime next week!"

"Sorry about that," Marjorie said, winking at Braden. If he thought he was getting her to himself for the afternoon, he had another think coming. "I had some urgent business and got quite caught up."

"That's fine," Cecelia said in a magnanimous tone completely unlike her. "I'm just relieved I didn't have to go an entire day without one of your wonderful coffees and scones. Not to mention a few minutes petting a ragdoll."

Chaplin's head jerked up, and he trotted over as though she'd called his name. "Steady on," Marjorie said with a laugh, feeling giggly. "At this rate, I'll have to bring over an adoption form."

"Oh, we're not there yet," Cecelia said, spraying hand sanitiser on her fingers and rubbing them briskly. "I think I'm destined to be like a kitten grandmother. Happy to visit but always leaving them with someone else at the end of the day."

"Oh, no." Marjorie stared out the side window in disbelief. "I swear, that kitten is driving me bonkers."

"What's that?" Braden walked over and stood behind her, one hand resting on her shoulder.

"Houdini." She pointed to his face staring out from Esme's window. "He's the whole reason I got in this mess today. How on earth does he escape all the time? I've been over the studio from top to toe and can't find how he gets in there."

"Do you want me to—"

"I'll get him," Marjorie said with a sigh, pulling off her apron. "Could you look after the till while I'm out? And serve up any customers."

"Leaving me in charge of the giant coffee

machine," Braden teased, tossing a wink towards Cecelia. "We all know what *that* means."

Marjorie retraced her steps from the morning, unlocking the back door and almost colliding with the stepladder. "We won't be needing you again," she said in an annoyed voice, folding it up and resting it against the wall.

In a louder voice, light and airy so the Chartreux wouldn't think she was upset, she said, "Esme's housed enough unwelcome guests this week without adding a naughty kitten."

She walked through to the massage room, scooping up Houdini before he could perform yet another magical escape.

A man thudded onto the floor behind her. Tyrone. Fletcher's legs wiggled as he tried to let himself down more gently through the trapdoor. A duffel bag was slung over his shoulder.

At once, Marjorie realised her mistake. Where else would Fletcher have hidden the drugs if not here? He could hardly have stashed them at home or in the submerged car. Anywhere else along his route back to the township would have left them prey to the elements.

"Let me go," she said in a small voice, cradling the kitten close to her chest. "I'll pretend I didn't see you."

"You won't need to pretend anything at all, doll." Tyrone strode a few steps towards her. "I've had enough of you poking your nose in."

"Hey, now. This is nothing to do with her," Fletcher called out. "Just let her go back to the café. You've got what you wanted." He pulled off the duffel bag and dropped it on the floor.

"What I wanted?" Tyrone spun on his heel, his face contorting into an expression of pure rage. "I wanted to keep doing business the way I had been. The way I should be now if my lookout had kept his mind on the job."

"It's not my fault the police were on your trail," Fletcher said, visibly trembling. "Giving you a two-minute warning they were on their way wouldn't solve your problems. They swooped on four houses simultaneously. You were so far onto their radar, they couldn't see anything else."

"Well, we'll never know because you didn't give us a chance." Tyrone edged towards Fletcher, pulling a switchblade from the back pocket of his jeans. "The one thing I hired you for—"

"You didn't hire me! You blackmailed me. And it wasn't one thing. I had to act as your lookout and store a multitude of drugs in my home. The place I lived in. If the police had raided me, I'd be looking at twenty years or more!"

"And you'd deserve it, you little rat."

"I'm not the rat in your organisation," Fletcher said in a tight voice. "If you want to know why the police knew about your entire organisation, you should look closer to home."

Tyrone lunged, the knife blade slicing through Fletcher's shirt and raising a thin line of dark red across his chest.

"Don't!" Marjorie called out, trying to

shelter the kitten and pull her phone out. "You can leave now. No one else needs to be hurt."

"But I want to hurt him," Tyrone growled. "I want to hurt him so bad."

"Yoo-hoo." Braden's face appeared through the back door. "Are you—?"

The joy fell off his face as he took in the scene in front of him. He tried to step back, but Tyrone skipped over and grabbed the front of his shirt, dragging him inside.

"Well, well. Looks like we're going to have a party," he said as a mean smile stretched his lips thin. "Is there anyone else on their way or is the gang all here?"

Holding the knife to Braden's throat, Tyrone manhandled him into the massage room, pushing him into the corner near Marjorie before shoving Fletcher inside to join them. He pulled open cupboards and drawers, throwing out a thin rope that Esme used to hang towels from on rainy days.

"Tie them up," he ordered Fletcher. "Nice and tight."

While Tyrone levelled the knife at him,

Fletcher did his bidding. Houdini jumped out of Marjorie's arms, appearing confused and retreating into a corner.

"Stiffen your muscles," Braden whispered out of the side of his mouth and she tensed her arms while Fletcher looped the rope around them. With so many loops and knots, she soon lost hope it would make any difference.

"Now, you. Back up against them."

Tyrone bound Fletcher's wrists then pulled the rope through until the three of them were back to back, tied tightly together.

"Not the best job in the world but it'll hold you long enough," he said, smashing a bottle of massage oil on the floor.

As he took a lighter out of his pocket, Marjorie understood he meant to set the room on fire. The ropes wouldn't hinder them for long, but with flames raging, they might not be able to beat the smoke.

"No," she cried out, struggling in earnest. "You can let us go. Nobody needs to know anything."

The faint creak from the back door leant her renewed hope. Hadn't Regina said she'd stop by? If that was her now, they just needed to keep him occupied a few minutes more and they might be rescued.

"What will it take to let us go?" she yelled, hoping to muffle the noise of footsteps. "We've got money. And cupcakes."

Tyrone slapped his knee and bent over laughing. "Cupcakes? Unless you're baking them with some extra ingredients, I don't think so."

When he stood up again, Cecelia slipped into the room behind him. She was rummaging in her purse, her face stricken.

Tyrone heard the noise and turned, receiving a spray of hand sanitiser straight in the eyes. While he yelled, temporarily blinded, Marjorie hauled herself and the roped companions over to him, kicking at his ankles.

He yelped and hopped on one foot, jumping backwards. Houdini shot forward, climbing up his body like he was a cat tree, and digging his claws into the man's face.

"Kick his legs out," Marjorie screamed as the roped trio twisted until she couldn't reach him. Braden grunted with effort and soon Tyrone was on the ground.

"He's got a knife!" Fletcher yelled at the astonished Cecelia. "In his front pocket!"

She reached down, quickly flicking it free, then standing and cutting through their ropes.

"No," Tyrone said, stumbling to his knees, blood and tears streaming down his face. "Wait…"

Regina hammered on the front door of the studio. "Police! Open up!"

Wrestling the cut ropes off her body, Marjorie undid the locks, opening the door to her friend. "The one on the floor," she said, pointing. "He's the head drug dealer."

Tyrone staggered to his feet, plucking Houdini off his head and throwing him into a corner. The nimble kitten landed on his feet, hissing and arching his back like a bow.

"Get back down on the floor," Regina

ordered, holding a taser out, ready to fire. "If I have to light you up, I will."

As multiple sirens heralded backup, Tyrone collapsed onto the floor, lacing his hands behind his neck as ordered. While Regina secured him with cuffs, Marjorie raced over to pick up Houdini, cradling his stiff body close.

Cecelia stared about her in wonder, a small frown creasing her face. "I just came over here to pay because no one was at the counter. Is this what goes on over here? I thought it was a massage place."

## CHAPTER SIXTEEN

Marjorie stood up and stretched out her back, feeling the knots in her spine pop into the right place, one by one. "It's been a long time since I've scrubbed a floor," she said in a mild complaint. "This is a younger woman's game."

Braden clambered to his feet and wrinkled his nose. "I've never done it before. I thought there were machines for this kind of stuff."

"Machines to get massage oil off polished floorboards? That's specific. At least it's not as bad as what we had to get out of the attic."

Marjorie's mouth twisted down at the corners. Fletcher's weeklong stay had left an unspeakable mess.

"They should've made him clean up after himself as punishment," Braden agreed, taking their buckets of dirty water outside to empty into the spouting drain. "Instead of just letting him go."

"No one let him go," Marjorie said in a slightly nettled tone. "He'll have to complete lots of community service, just under a different name."

"Yeah. Cleaning counts as community service, doesn't it?"

"Drop it," Marjorie said, laughing. "Honestly, we're all alive and well, apart from a few bruised knees and aching backs. We got off lightly."

There was a honk from outside, and Marjorie walked into the carpark to see Duncan grinning at her from the driver's seat. He'd come through his kidnapping adventure relatively unscathed, although she wondered how well he'd sleep at night for the coming few months.

"I'd like to introduce you to my parents," Duncan said, opening the back door so an older version of himself could emerge with a smiling woman at his side. "This is Marjorie," he said to his folks. "She's the real hero of the hour."

"It's nice to meet you," Sheryl Byrne said, nudging her husband Allan in the ribs until he agreed.

"Lovely to meet you, too," Marjorie replied, shaking their hands. "Although I'm afraid it's not under the best circumstances."

"Don't need to say that twice," Allan grumbled. "We spent twenty hours on a plane thinking our son was dead only to land and find out he's a jackass."

"Language!" his wife said, giving him a stern look as a reprimand.

"Ha! That's nothing as bad as what I want to call him."

"Fletcher seemed very nice outside of all

the bad stuff," Marjorie said, feeling upset she couldn't teleport back to that time.

"Let's hope he makes it back to that state," Duncan said, then turned to his parents. "Do you want a cup of tea or coffee before we go? This place has the best pinwheel scones."

"Oh, go on. Twist my arm." Sheryl gave a nod to Marjorie and headed inside, cooing with delight when a kitten met her by the door.

"We'd better not end up with one of those in the next seat on the way home," Allan growled. "You know your mother and animals."

He stomped off after his wife, leaving Duncan making an apologetic face. "They're usually easier to get along with. The flight's knocked it out of them."

"Not to mention, thinking their son was dead for the whole trip." Marjorie touched Duncan's upper arm. "They seem lovely. Why don't you go in and I'll catch up in a minute?"

"I'll take that as my cue to leave," Braden said,

leaning over to give her a soft kiss on the lips before hooking empty buckets over his arms and grabbing hold of the broom and mop. "How about we plan something nice for this weekend? There's a festival in Kaikoura I can get you back from in time for your afternoon bedtime."

"Sounds good," she said, rolling her eyes at the jest. "I'll pack a picnic lunch for the trip there."

As she waved goodbye, a familiar car pulled onto the road at the base of the hill. Esme and Jerry.

"What are you two doing back here so soon?" she asked as they pulled into the shared car park. "I thought you had another week booked away."

"When Hanmer is heaving with excitement?" Esme jumped out and spun in a circle. "It doesn't look any different from when we left but according to the police, it's been non-stop action."

"They called you?" Marjorie gave her friend a hug as she tried to cover up her disappointment. "And here I was trying to spin the whole thing into an amusing anecdote to tell you over dinner when you returned."

"You can still do that," Jerry said, shaking her hand and clapping her on the shoulder. "In fact, since I've lost my holiday, I might plan a few dinner parties. Are you still hooked up with that weird computer engineer or should I call around a few of my single friends?"

"I'm still with Braden if that's what you're asking," Marjorie said with a laugh. "And please don't introduce me to any more single men. One is quite enough."

"Isn't that your kitten making a run for it?" Esme said, pointing over Jerry's shoulder.

"Houdini! You get back here right this minute!"

They gave chase, the kitten easily escaping their clutches until they could barely move from laughing. Duncan wandered outside, presumably to check where the café host was, and Houdini trotted straight up to him, nuzzling against the leg of his jeans like it was a long-lost friend.

"Are you causing trouble, little man?" he said, picking the Chartreux cat up and placing it against his chest. "You're a scamp, aren't you?"

"Have you been cleaning?" Esme asked, opening the back door to the massage rooms and sniffing. "It smells like lemon and disinfectant."

"That's exactly right." Marjorie walked over and steered her friend towards the café. "But come inside here, first. Have a seat and a coffee and we can talk all about what happened while you were gone."

"Why's the back door open while the front door's locked?" Jerry asked, ever practical.

"Oh, no." Marjorie put a hand over her mouth as it dropped open in horror. "I never got the key back off Fletcher. I'm so sorry."

"Oh, honey. Don't worry. After what the police told me, I've already ordered a locksmith to meet me bright and early tomorrow morning." Esme glanced back at her business. "I'd also ordered a cleaning crew, but it appears somebody beat me to that task."

"It's the least I could do."

Inside, Duncan played catch the feather with Houdini while Cecelia pressed a napkin to the corners of her mouth, finishing up with her mid-morning treat.

"I told you, it's on the house," Marjorie protested as she sidled up to the counter with a strange expression on her face. "After your help with Tyrone, I need some way to pay you back."

"Oh, it would've all turned out okay," Cecelia said, dismissing the thanks with one hand while her pleased smile accepted the compliment. "And I was after a form if you've got one handy."

"I do." Marjorie passed over a clipboard and pen, trying not to show her astonishment.

"This isn't a promise or anything," Cecelia warned, wiggling the pen up and down. "But I thought it would be nice to see if I meet the criteria. If I ever want to."

"Sure." Marjorie nodded as though trial-runs happened every day. "And you know, once I have a passed inspection on file from the SPCA, it's not a final obligation."

"Exactly," Cecelia agreed, turning and speaking to Chaplin. "It's just a possibility if we both think we could work together."

It was the first time owning a kitten had been phrased as work, but Marjorie couldn't help glowing as the prim woman sat down with the clipboard, taking each question with studious concentration.

"Here you go," she said a few minutes later, taking plates of goodies out to the Byrne family. "Are you staying in town long?"

"No longer than we can help it," Allan muttered darkly, pulling a black coffee close and stirring in five sugars in quick succession.

"Dad!"

"Well, we're not."

"You don't have to put it like that. It's hardly the town's fault Fletcher is an idiot."

"Duncan!" This time it was Sheryl's turn to protest. "Speak nicely about your brother or don't speak about him at all."

"That'll mean no one ever mentions his name again." Allan took a sip of coffee and followed it up with a huge bite of a pinwheel scone. "Oh, these are good."

"Told you." Duncan appeared as pleased as if he'd baked them himself. "And what are you staring at me for, little fellow?"

Houdini put his front paws on the young man's leg, taking two goes before he could jump up into his lap.

"Oh, isn't he sweet?" Sheryl squealed.

"Six months quarantine," Allan said, munching through the rest of his treat as though it had done him a personal injury. "That's what you're looking at for importing animals."

"Not for a little kitten, surely."

"You're not to adopt a cat! Do you hear me?" Allan sat back, draining the rest of his coffee, though it must be hot enough to burn his mouth. "They have cats in Europe."

"Not this one," Duncan said, lifting him up and rubbing his nose. "But I agree. You don't need a kitten. And neither do I."

He set the Chartreux down on the floor and set to work on his own scone and coffee. After a minute of being ignored, the kitten mewed plaintively and jumped into Duncan's lap again.

"Why're you looking at me like that for?" Duncan asked, raising his eyebrows. "I've already told you I'm not adopting a kitten so you can drop the attitude."

Houdini mewed again, then curled into a ball and fell asleep while Duncan's stern expression melted into one of pure love.

Marjorie reached under the counter for another adoption form. No matter the protestations, she could tell when a kitten had stolen a man's heart.

**_Thank you for taking the time to read Chartreux Shock._**

**_If you enjoyed it, please consider telling your friends or posting a short review. Word of_**

*mouth is an author's best friend, and much appreciated.*

*Thank you, again. Katherine Hayton.*

## Next up in Marjorie's Cozy Kitten Café: Lykoi Larceny

# ALSO BY KATHERINE HAYTON

Chartreux Shock (Marjorie's Cozy Kitten Café)

Calico Confusion (Marjorie's Cozy Kitten Café)

Charity Shop Haunted Mysteries – Books 1-3

Miss Hawthorne Sits for a Spell (Charity Shop Haunted Mystery)

Mr Wilmott Gets Old School (Charity Shop Haunted Mystery)

Mrs Pettigrew Sees a Ghost (Charity Shop Haunted Mystery)

A Bed for Suite Dreams (A Hotel Inspector Cozy Mystery)

A Stay With Reservations (A Hotel Inspector Cozy Mystery)

A Job of Inn Dependence (A Hotel Inspector Cozy Mystery)

The Double Dip (Honeybee Cozy Mystery)

The Honey Trap (Honeybee Cozy Mystery)

The Buzz Kill (Honeybee Cozy Mystery)

Tea Shop Cozy Mysteries – Books 1-6

Hibiscus Homicide (Tea Shop Cozy Mystery)

Keeping Mums (Tea Shop Cozy Mystery)

Orange Juiced (Tea Shop Cozy Mystery)

Deathbed of Roses (Tea Shop Cozy Mystery)

Berry Murderous (Tea Shop Cozy Mystery)

Pushing Up Daisies (Tea Shop Cozy Mystery)

Food Bowl Mysteries – Books 1-3

You're Kitten Me (Food Bowl Mysteries)

Cat Red-Handed (Food Bowl Mysteries)

An Impawsible Situation (Food Bowl Mysteries)

The Sweet Baked Mysteries - Books 1-6

Cinnamon and Sinfulness (Sweet Baked Mystery)

Raspberries and Retaliation (Sweet Baked Mystery)

Pumpkin Spice & Poisoning (Sweet Baked Mystery)

Blueberries and Bereavement (Sweet Baked Mystery)

Strawberries and Suffering (Sweet Baked Mystery)

Cupcakes and Conspiracies (Sweet Baked Mystery)

The Only Secret Left to Keep (Detective Ngaire Blakes)

The Second Stage of Grief (Detective Ngaire Blakes)

The Three Deaths of Magdalene Lynton (Detective Ngaire Blakes)

Christchurch Crime Thriller Boxset

Breathe and Release (A Christchurch Crime Thriller)

Skeletal (A Christchurch Crime Thriller)

Found, Near Water (A Christchurch Crime Thriller)

# ABOUT THE AUTHOR

Katherine Hayton is a middle-aged woman who works in insurance, doesn't have children or pets, can't drive, has lived in Christchurch her entire life, and currently resides a two-minute walk from where she was born.

For some reason, she's developed a rich fantasy life.

www.katherinehayton.com

Made in the USA
Columbia, SC
10 December 2019